THE
CELLAR

THE CELLAR

A. J. WHITTEN

Houghton Mifflin Harcourt

Boston   New York   2011

www.hmhbooks.com

Text set in Adobe Garamond Pro

Library of Congress Cataloging-in-Publication Data
Whitten, A. J.
The cellar / A.J. Whitten.—1st ed.
p. cm.
Summary: Seventeen-year-old Meredith Willis has seen the monstrous truth about
her new next-door neighbor, Adrien, who is wildly popular at school and her sister
Heather's new love interest, but trying to stop him could be fatal.
ISBN 978-0-547-23253-9
[1. Zombies—Fiction. 2. Supernatural—Fiction. 3. Sisters—Fiction. 4. High
schools—Fiction. 5. Schools—Fiction. 6. Theater—Fiction. 7. Dating
(Social customs)—Fiction.] I. Title.
PZ7.W617829Cel 2011
[Fic]—dc22
2010027452

Manufactured in the United States of America
DOC 10 9 8 7 6 5 4 3 2 1

4500285064

CHAPTER 1

"Some days, Meredith, I just . . . I just wish it was me who died," my sister said that Tuesday morning in early September.

I stared at Heather. At sixteen she was a younger version of me, with darker hair and browner eyes. I was only ten months older than her but some days felt like a decade older.

I must have heard her wrong. She talked so softly now, I was always hearing something other than what she really said. "You . . . you what?"

"I just said I wish it had been me. That's all." Heather shrugged. Then she poured a crapload of Cocoa Pebbles into the new white bowls Mom had bought the week before. They were ridiculously giant bowls. One day my mother brought them home and, two seconds later, threw out all our old dishes. The ones I really liked, the yellow ones with the blue flowers, the same ones I'd been eating out of since I was four.

That's what she did now. Spend money. In the past six months she'd bought a lot of things we didn't need. I was sure her Visa was going to start smoking at any second. A psychiatrist would have a lot of really good analysis for why.

Too bad the only shrink my mother went to see was named Neiman Marcus.

Our Aunt Evelyn, my mother's older sister, had moved in six weeks ago with her twin sons and taken over as mom. She was the one who made dinner, who did the laundry, who pecked over us like a worried hen all day. Her twin boys—Ted and Tad, but we called them Tweedledee and Tweedledum because we were pretty sure they shared a solitary brain cell—didn't do much more than go to school and play basketball. They were both seniors and already had full rides to some midwest university that liked them dumb, tall, and able to dribble. They had already left for school that morning, probably for one of their early scrimmages.

"Pass the milk, will you?" Heather said.

I held on to the two-percent. It was pretty much the only thing I had a hold on right now. My life, which used to seem so perfect, had become totally distorted. Everything I'd thought meant something—my friends, yearbook, school—now rang empty and cold. I kept waiting for some normalcy to come back, like the tulips my dad and I had planted in the front yard last year. Except the squirrels stole the bulbs, and only three of the twenty pink flowers encored.

Maybe it was a sign. Like those big yellow billboards on the highway screaming at you to lose fifty pounds or quit smoking. The signs you ignore until it's too late and all of a sudden, you're lying in a hospital bed, on the wrong end of a scalpel.

I pushed away my cereal. Wished Aunt Evelyn hadn't gone to her Bible study this morning so we could have had bacon and eggs instead. Maybe then Heather wouldn't have been in such a weird mood. "Heather, you can't just say something like that. I mean . . ."

"What?" She let out a sigh and sat back, turning her face away. When she did, the long curtain of her brown hair shifted slightly, exposing the scar that ran from her forehead to her chin, as if her face had been cut in half.

It almost had. By a four-door sedan that had crumpled like a tuna can.

Leaving Heather a bloody mess, and killing Dad.

In two seconds, the Willis family had gone from being typical suburbanites—mom, dad, two daughters, living in a four-bedroom ranch—to a tragic statistic. The psychiatrist we talked to would quote numbers at me and Heather, as though that would make us feel better. As if being part of a group of one point five gazillion kids whose parents had been killed in car accidents in the past two decades was some kind of top one hundred Facebook group we should join.

"What were you going to say?" Heather asked.

I opened my mouth, but nothing wise came pouring out. If I'd had anything smart to say, I'd have said it six months ago, when Heather was lying in a hospital bed and my mother was standing in a funeral home picking out a casket.

So I passed the milk. We sat there and ate in silence.

Ever since the "incident"—which was what everyone called it, as if one innocuous word could turn the crappiest day of our lives into something more palatable, like throwing cheese on broccoli—Heather had fallen into a dark pit. The perfect student had to be dragged to school. To soccer practice, where she was about as useful as a shrub in the middle of the field.

I'd become the star student. Me, the one who had barely passed Geometry, and that was only because I'd begged Mr. Sanders to have mercy on me. Instead of my mom pushing us to be on the honor roll, my crappy C average became the new norm in our house. Yearbook layouts became the talk around the table, because I was the only one talking about what I did. Not that Mom plugged in any better than a faulty toaster, but at least we were all here.

Existing.

Yeah, that was what I'd call it. Existing in a bubble of silence, punctuated with the scraping of spoons against stupid, huge bowls.

What we needed more than anything right now was something new. Something big. Something to wake us up.

A movement outside the window caught my eye. A flash of red. The roar of an engine starting. I put down my spoon and crossed to the window. In the next driveway, gray smoke curled out of the exhaust pipe of a cherry red Camaro, one of those sports cars that screamed, *Look at me!* I hated those things because they made stupid people drive too fast and take risks that caused accidents that shouldn't have happened otherwise. Behind the wheel sat a guy dressed in black, tall and thin, wearing sunglasses. White ruffle-edged curtains that hadn't been there yesterday hung in the windows of the two-story Victorian, and a wicker rocker sat on the porch. "Hey, when did someone move into the house next door?"

"Mer, that place has been abandoned for as long as we've lived here. Mom can't *give* that place away." Our mother was a real estate agent. Her trademark sign said BRINGING YOU AND YOURS HOME, now wasn't on the lawn next door anymore. The house next door had been one of her few failures. Old and rundown, left to rot by the old lady who'd lived there for, like, five hundred years, the place hadn't sold or been rented in years. "Who would want that piece of crap?"

"Well, somebody did. And now they're living there. Look." I pointed out the window.

Heather let out another sigh—sighing had become her thing lately—and got to her feet, slowly. She shuffled over to the window, pretended to look, then turned away.

"You didn't look."

"I did."

"You didn't." I grabbed her arm, spun her around, and held her at the window until she actually raised her head and looked past her wall of hair. "Look. People."

"Not 'people.' One person." She huffed. "Big deal. I'm going to school."

Again, she'd shut me out. I shouldn't care or let it bother me. It wasn't as if I didn't have my own problems, but still, every time she did that, a knife ran through my heart. As I turned from the window, I caught sight of my father's fishing cap, tucked high on top of the fridge. Forgotten and dusty. But for a second, it was as though he were still there.

I opened my mouth to tell Heather, but she had already turned away, sending a clear message. She was done. With me, with conversation.

Heather walked out the door—not waiting for me, not

that she ever did anymore—and I did something I never used to do.

I prayed for a miracle. For something to bring my sister back to the land of the living.

CHAPTER 2

The halls closed in around Heather Willis, the passing students becoming a human pressure cooker. She drew her arms in against herself, trying to become small, invisible, to avoid contact. Avoid talking.

Wanting to be invisible. Gone.

"Heather!" From a classroom across the hall, Alicia Smallwood waved her arm big, wide, way too enthusiastically. Heather sent her a half nod but didn't move. Alicia's hand fell away, her face dropped into a frown, and she headed into English.

The hall began to drain. In a few seconds, she'd have to go inside Mrs. Fisher's class, take a quiz she was going to fail. Or she could just stand here. What was the point, really, in going to class? In doing any of it anymore?

"You look lost," a deep voice said from behind her. "Like me."

Heather turned, about to blast whoever was bothering her this time. She stopped. Stared.

At the very guy who had moved in next door to her. From far away this morning, she hadn't seen any details, but now—

Oh, now she did.

Up close, he was . . . gorgeous. Dark hair, a bit long in the back, just enough to curl over his collar, long dark jeans, a black suit jacket, something no other guy would have dared to wear over a white T, untucked. He wore sunglasses—not Ray-Bans, but something very similar and very . . . mysterious. They reflected back her face, the shock in her eyes.

He was hot.

And he was looking at her.

Waiting for her to say something. She took a breath. Swallowed. Opened her mouth finally. "You're—"

"New here. And looking for a friend." He grinned. When he did, the cloud in Heather's chest lifted.

And for the first time in six months, she felt as though she had something to look forward to.

*   *   *

"OH MY GOD, MEREDITH, HAVE YOU SEEN HIM?" Cassidy charged me like a freight train, arms waving, eyes wide. I'd known Cassidy Cramer since second grade, and she'd always talked in caps—loud and as if every event were worthy of a megaphone.

It was why she'd been made cheerleading squad captain. No one could rah-rah better than Cass. And when the cheerleaders were all lacking a little in the enthusiasm department, Cass more than made up for it with her happy screams. So when she came roaring at me, I didn't think it was anything out of the ordinary and just shrugged.

Mr. DeLue hadn't shown up for World History yet, which meant if I was smart, I'd take the extra minutes to study for the quiz.

Uh, yeah. Not.

I sat down next to Cassidy. "Seen who?"

"The new guy! He is SO CUTE. Like Ashton Kutcher and Zac Efron, with a bit of David Beckham. He could be a MODEL, honest. OH MY GOD, Meredith. Tell me you saw him."

"New guy?" It took me a second, and then I made the connection. "I bet he's the guy who moved in next door to me. Does he drive a Camaro?"

Cassidy nodded. "It's cherry, too. Color and condition. Everything about him is H-O-T."

In my back pocket, my cell vibrated. Once, twice, three, four times, texts pouring in. I slid it out, dropped down in my seat in case Mr. DeLue walked in, and checked the messages. "New Guy Alert: OMG." "Who's got hot guy in class? Tell! I'll hit Guid. up & switch!!" "Get his digits! Does he have a FB page?"

Apparently everyone had seen him—and the opinion was unanimous. You'd think nothing ever happened here. Okay, so nothing did. Pretty sad, though, that one new guy could create a bigger stir than a presidential election.

Krystal and Paula slid into their seats behind us, plopping their books under their seats, where we all knew they'd stay the entire class. We took history because we had to. Didn't mean we had to participate. "What are we talking about?" Krystal asked.

"New guy," Cass said. "Have you seen him?"

"Have I seen him?" Krystal put a hand over her heart. "I 'bout died when I did. He is frosting on a stick."

Paula nodded so hard, her platinum blond ponytail nearly took out her left eye. "The entire squad followed him down the hall, trying to talk to him, but he was, like, mystery guy. All smiles, no talk. Hey, think we can convince him to be our mascot?"

"You want him to put on the bear costume and run around the field?" I asked.

"Hell, no. I want to keep him in the locker room." Paula grinned. "For inspiration."

Cassidy laughed. "Maybe we can convince Mrs. Lewis that we need him for inspiration in gym. You know, to get us to do more pushups or laps. I know *I'd* run to him."

"Mrs. Lewis *is* legally blind," Paula said. "We'll tell her the new guy is a chick with a butch cut."

Cassidy raised a hand and slapped Paula a high-five. "Brilliant."

Krystal shook her head. "Way to start a catfight in the locker room. Already, every girl in school wants him."

"You don't think he's a little"—I paused—"over the top? You know, trying too hard with the sunglasses and the fast car."

The other girls stared at me as if I was crazy. "Uh, no," Cassidy said.

I shook my head and waited for the conversation about the new guy to die down.

"You want to get some burgers after school?" Paula asked after a while, finally done talking about Hottie McHotpants. "I don't have cheer till four."

"Can't," I said. "I have an eye doctor appointment."

"You doing okay with that?" Paula asked, her voice quiet.

"Yeah, yeah. Everything's great." *Liar.*

Just after the final bell rang, Mr. DeLue came rushing in the door, trailing papers from his briefcase like Hansel leaving a trail of bread crumbs. On the way to his desk, he mumbled under his breath something about forgetting the pencils. Then he stopped, scratched his head, which puffed his thick, unruly white hair into a fuzzy cotton ball, and stared at all of us as though he couldn't figure out why we were there. "Oh, yes. The test."

"*Quiz*, Mr. DeLue," Kurt Lessing called from the second row. "Don't mess with my chill by changing it to a test."

"Yes, yes, quiz." He scratched his head again and turned a few times. "Now, where—"

"Look under your arm," Wendell Marks said, getting up to point out the papers fluttering beneath Mr. DeLue's elbow.

Kurt smacked Wendell in the back of the head. "Shut. Up."

Mr. DeLue lifted his arm and smiled, as if he'd just found gold in his bellybutton. "Well, there you go. Quiz, people. On World War One. Take your seats."

Thirty-two students shot Wendell visual death rays. There were several muttered "moron"s and a few other less flattering words sent Wendell's way. He ignored them, sitting in his front and center seat, pencil at the ready. In kindergarten,

Wendell Marks had been my Play-Doh buddy. No one could make a blue snowman like Wendell.

He'd also been the one who talked me into giving him a kiss in the coat closet after recess. A real wild child, that Wendell. You'd never know it now.

Mr. DeLue started passing out the quizzes. "Eyes on your own papers. Bring your quiz to me when you're finished. Homework for today is on the board. That's the only thing I want to see you working on if you finish ear—"

The classroom door opened. Everyone except Wendell stopped listening to Mr. DeLue and turned toward the door. Paula and Krystal sucked in a breath at the same time.

Cassidy leaned over and smacked me on the arm. "He's *here*."

He was the guy from the Camaro, my new next-door neighbor. Tall, broad shouldered, with the kind of lanky, confident walk that said he knew his place in the world and didn't care what anyone thought about him. His dark hair— so dark it looked black—was long enough for a little pony- tail, but he'd let it curl over the collar of his suit jacket, the kind that looked custom-made, fitted just to his body. He had on sunglasses—even though he was inside and anything that wasn't prescription was *verboten* according to school dress code.

Yeah, as if we all read and followed school dress code. Most of us liked to think of it as a working guideline for apparel.

"Do you see him?" Cassidy whispered, the only one talking. Everyone else seemed to be in some temporary trance, staring at the new kid as if he'd stepped out of a UFO. Especially the girls. As he walked through the classroom, he seemed to have a way of smiling at every girl individually, and when he did, each became transfixed. Mute. The guys, not so much, but they still seemed to be sizing up their new competition.

My phone started buzzing again. Word spread faster than cold germs here.

Mr. DeLue was the first to clear his throat. "Welcome, welcome, Mr. . . . ?"

"St. Germain. Adrien St. Germain."

His words had an almost lyrical accent. French? Spanish? I couldn't tell, and my foreign language skills weren't much better than my geometry. Either way, he wasn't from around here.

"Well, Mr. St. Germain, please take a seat." Mr. DeLue looked down and scribbled in his planner while he talked. "The class is taking a test—"

"*Quiz*, Mr. D.," Kurt corrected.

"Quiz, but you're welcome to join the class as soon as we're done. I'll go get you a . . ." Mr. DeLue paused and looked up from his planner. "A, um . . ."

A long, slow smile spread across Adrien's face. Not the kind that said Mr. DeLue had all the brains of a space monkey, but the patient, cool-with-me-dude kind. "A book, sir?"

The "sir" at the end got Mr. DeLue's attention. Poor guy probably hadn't been called that since *T. rexes* roamed the earth. "Yes, yes, a book. Now, if I could just remember where . . ."

Adrien jerked his chin, a millimeter, maybe two, in the direction of the bookshelf under the window. Mr. DeLue nodded and hurried over, grabbing a copy of the thick *World History*. Adrien took it with a careless grin, then plopped into the nearest seat.

Beside me.

On my opposite side, Cassidy smacked my arm again. As though I'd betrayed her by not shoving Adrien into the empty slot on her left—next to the air conditioner that blew hot air no matter the weather. Paula and Krystal sighed together. Then they stared at Adrien. Hard and intensely.

"Hey!" I whispered to Cassidy. "You're going to leave a mark."

She scowled. "You deserved it. I have an empty desk and an empty space in my heart."

I rolled my eyes and went back to my quiz.

1. What was the Triple Alliance? Who were its members?

I could feel him staring at me. Even though my head was down, my eyes on the paper in front of me. I snuck a glance over my shoulder. Adrien leaned back against the hard plastic chair, one arm draped over the side, the other cradling the opened textbook. He looked—to anyone but me—as if he was reading all about America's conquest during the war.

Except . . .

There was something behind those sunglasses. Something I could feel. I couldn't see it, but I knew—

Knew there was more.

I blinked, rubbed at my eyes. They were acting up, that was all.

Adrien tipped his chin up and gave me a slow smile. Our gazes met—my brown eyes, his shaded ones—and a shiver ran down my spine. The kind of shiver that was full of awareness, of OMG, HE'S LOOKING AT ME. My breath caught in my throat, and my heart skipped a beat.

Mr. DeLue cleared his throat. "Miss Willis? Eyes on the test."

Kurt let out a long-suffering sigh. "Quiz, Mr. D."

I jerked back to attention. Adrien's grin widened, teasing me because I'd been caught staring, and then he dropped his gaze to the book again.

As he did, the sunglasses slid a little lower on his face. In an instant, he reached up to push them back, the movement so swift, probably no one but me saw it.

Or saw what was behind those sunglasses.

A flicker of something. I wasn't sure what, because it was so fast that I was sure I'd imagined it. Because for a second there, I thought I'd seen—

Squirming white worms, twisting in and out of empty skull sockets. Instead of pupils, two thick black-skinned beetles, their tiny legs riding the worms. Then, just as fast as I'd seen them—had I seen them at all?—they were gone, covered by his sunglasses.

Yeah, no way. That was crazy. A trick of the crappy overhead fluorescent lights that kept flickering. Or maybe my eyes were dry. The doctor had said that someday, my condition would get bad and my vision would start to tank. I fumbled in my back pocket for my prescription eye drops and squirted some into each eye.

I must have made up the whole thing. No one alive could have eyes like that. I'd been dreaming. Distracted. Operating on a sugar rush from the Cocoa Pebbles.

I glanced over at Adrien again and saw a guy as normal as anyone else. He gave me a lopsided grin, as sure-footed as a lion on the prairie, then dropped one finger down and—

Pointed it right at me. Bull's-eye.

CHAPTER 3

Outside the house, the vulture and the crows waited. The sexton beetles waited. The flies hovered, waiting. And far away, hidden in an abandoned building's shadows, the hyenas waited.

Raw hunger stirred inside the beasts. They paced. They watched for the signal from the one who fed them. They had followed him here, followed him everywhere he went. He was their master, the one to whom they had pledged their loyalty. For that, he rewarded them. Very well.

Soon, he had promised, there would be a feast—a feast unlike any of the others before. Piles and piles of bones and fat and gristle to devour. Enough to feed them all, many times over. With him in charge, they would eat well, he had said. Be treated as partners, not as annoyances.

Not the way *she* had treated them.

The animals paced. And anticipated. Fresh meat. The sweetest meal of all. And it would be theirs to have. Soon.

CHAPTER 4

He wants you," Cassidy said in the hall. Paula and Krystal had already headed off to meet up with the rest of the female pop and, I was sure, relate every moment of the new guy's time in our class. I could already hear the excited shrieks from where I was standing. What was it about that guy? He'd set off a feeding frenzy in school.

Okay, so he was cute. Really cute. But there were tons of cute guys in the world. Okay, maybe not in my world at Jefferson High School in western Massachusetts, but still . . . it wasn't as though he were part of the endangered species list or anything.

And so what if I'd felt a shiver when he'd smiled at me? I wasn't fainting at his feet like everyone else. I just didn't get the whole this-guy-is-Superman-and-supermodel-all-in-one thing. Maybe it was because he wasn't my type. At all. He seemed kind of showy and into himself. I hated that.

"He wants you bad, you traitor," Cassidy added.

For a second in Mr. DeLue's class, the idea of Camaro guy wanting me had been . . .

Thrilling. Exciting. Cool.

I mean, who wouldn't find that cool? Except the last thing I needed right now was a relationship. Someone else who needed something from me. I didn't have enough energy to take care of an English Ivy, never mind a boyfriend. "He does not. And besides, I don't want him."

Cassidy let out a whoosh of disbelief. "Are you kidding me? I saw you staring at him like you were starving and he was the last egg roll at the all-you-can-eat Chinese buffet."

I started toward my locker. "What is that supposed to mean?"

Cassidy slipped in between me and my combination. "Face it, Meredith, you think he's hot, too. And when he pointed at you"—she pressed a hand to her chest—"it made *me* melt. How lucky can you get, having that guy live next door to you? It's, like, a total advantage over anyone else. So, now I hate you. In fact, I think Krystal and Paula do, too. We're going to start a club."

I could hear Cassidy was only half kidding.

I twirled the wheel to the right, then left. What was the combination, again? For Pete's sake, I'd had the same locker for two years, and now I couldn't remember three simple numbers? "Cass, you can have him. There's something . . . odd about him."

Cassidy pressed a hand to my forehead. "Maybe odd about you. Hot guy wants you, and you're handing him off?" She shrugged. "I'll take him, even if he's your leftovers."

The warning bell rang. "I better book it," Cassidy said. "Catch you at lunch?"

I switched World History for Spanish, then shut my locker. "Sure." Cassidy gave me a quick hug, then disappeared in the sea of high school bodies.

I shoved my way through the cattle chute that led to the foreign language hall, saying hey to a few people, but really, thinking more about that weird thing that had just happened in Mr. DeLue's class when Adrien's sunglasses had moved. The more distance I put between me and the history room, the more I convinced myself I'd imagined the whole thing or that it had just been my eyes acting up. I'd thought that kind of thing was supposed to happen years down the road. Or maybe I was going crazy.

Ever since the "incident," I hadn't slept well. When the sandman refused to pay me a visit, I stayed up late, watching horror movies on HBO. I'd seen them all, from the original *Friday the 13th* to the creepy *The Hills Have Eyes*. OD'ed on too many watchings of *The Ring* and *Drag Me to Hell*. In between, I devoured horror novels. I loved the whole feeling of being scared, of seeing the monsters die at the end. It was something about how *un*believable the horror films were. They were twenty steps away from the all-too-real horror I'd already lived, so I kept on watching and reading the fake stuff. It was easier than dealing with reality.

To be honest, I was surprised I hadn't seen snakes slithering out of my wall long before this thing with Adrien and his eyes. Dr. Howard, the shrink my mom took me to a couple times after my dad died, had said to expect a few nightmares. Some "residual effects" from the trauma, or whatever.

Yeah, that's what today had been. Too many movies, too much emotional baggage dropping onto my mental carousel at the same time.

Just as I turned the corner to the foreign language wing, Tweedledee and Tweedledum came up to me. "Yo, Meredith," one of them said—I could never remember who was who because they dressed alike, as if they were still five. Today, it was matching red and white striped shirts over white Ts and Levi's jeans. "Have you met that new guy?"

I nodded. God, was anyone going to talk about anything else?

"I don't like him," the other Tweedle said. "He totally dissed us this morning."

"Dissed you? How?"

Tweedledee leaned in close to me, looking around before he spoke. "Okay," he said, as if I were coming into the middle of a conversation, "so he's in our homeroom, and after the bell rings, Coach comes by to do basketball sign-ups, so me and Tad think we'll be nice, ask the new guy to join the team. You know, play Mr. Rogers."

"Mr. Rogers?"

"Be a good neighbor."

"Oh."

"So I go up to him and ask, 'Hey, what position do you play?' Cuz I'm thinking we need some warm bodies on the team, especially some as tall as him. And this new dude, he looks at me and Tad like we're pond scum. He waves his hand like this"—Tweedledee—Ted, I realized—demonstrated, making it look as if he were brushing dirt off his chest—"and then he walked away."

"Jerk," Tad said.

"Jerk," Ted echoed.

"Maybe he just doesn't like basketball."

"I don't know. I heard from Nate Wilkins that Adrien was asking about us. He said the guy called us 'those idiots who live next door.'" Ted put out his hands. "What's up with that?"

"Yeah," Tad said. "He doesn't know us well enough to call us idiots."

"Ain't that the truth," I muttered.

"We're going to keep an eye on him," Tweedledee said. "Don't know who he thinks he is, moving in here and acting like that. He keeps it up, we'll straighten him out."

Tweedledum nodded, and then they walked off, talking about how they'd show the new guy the best way to fit in. Sounded as though they planned on using their fists as demonstration props.

I shook my head, then started down the hall in the opposite direction. There were days when I seriously wondered if the Tweedle Twins and I all came from the same DNA pool.

Sam Cohen fell into step beside me. "Hey, Mer. How's it going?"

I looked up and saw his familiar blue eyes and the light wavy brown hair that needed a haircut but still managed to look pretty decent. He had on jeans and a blue checkered button-down shirt that he'd left open over a Nine Inch Nails T.

"Hey, Sam." He was really tall, which meant craning my head to look up at him, but that was okay. I liked Sam. He had a goofy, warm personality that said you could sit down over a pizza and ask him why guys were such losers—and he'd tell you the truth.

"So," he said, then after pausing a second, "how's Heather?"

Whenever Sam asked about Heather, he got this pained look on his face. Sam and Heather had dated for nine months—until the incident—and then she'd cut him off cold turkey. Not a word.

Now Sam came to me for info. Problem was, I didn't have any.

"Pretty much the same," I said.

"She ask about me?"

I wanted to lie, I really did. If only to get that beaten puppy look off his face. But I couldn't lie, no matter how much I tried. "No, she hasn't. Sorry, Sam."

He nodded again. "It's okay. I'll catch you at yearbook later." He started to head into his class, across the hall from mine, his shoulders weighed down.

I had a sudden urge to comfort him. I grabbed his arm. "Hey, wanna grab a burger after school one of these days? We could catch up. Talk like we used to when you hung around our house like a bad cold."

He turned back. For a second, I thought he'd say no and keep going with his shoulders hunched and that beaten puppy face. "Yeah, I would, Meredith." He smiled. "I really would."

A whoosh of something odd rose in my chest at his smile.

Something I'd never felt before. Something like—well, like *liking* him.

As I ducked into Spanish, a load of guilt came with me. I hadn't done anything wrong, but I could feel the potential for wrongness sitting right there. Sam was Heather's boyfriend, and the last thing in the world I wanted was to hurt her. This was *Sam*. I'd known him so long, he was practically a relative. When I saw Sam, I'd make that clear.

As I sat down, I caught a glimpse of Adrien walking down the hall. No, not walking—gliding, it seemed, with a female entourage twittering behind him. At the end of the hall, the Tweedle Twins glared, but Adrien didn't notice. He also didn't give any of his insta-harem a second glance. Instead, he turned toward me and smiled. Not a friendly how-you-doing-neighbor smile. Not a hey-I-know-you-from-history smile, either.

No, this was an I-know-your-secrets smile. And his smile said he was prepared to use them if he needed to.

A chill chased up my spine and stayed there the rest of the day.

CHAPTER 5

Once upon a time, there used to be four of them. Now there were only two.

They stood together by the window, watching. The only sound in the house came from the aquariums on the far wall. Two tanks, both large, the filters humming, the fish swimming back and forth, back and forth, waiting to be fed.

"Did you choose one yet, Adrien?" Marie asked. The tall, dark-haired woman beside him was not his mother, but over the past ninety years Adrien had come to think of her in that role. Not with love, but with the kind of understanding that came with someone who tended to his needs—not that he had many. But she was there and had been from the day he'd been awakened.

She'd helped him escape from the farm in Haiti where both of them had been raised from the dead for one purpose—to be slaves and work the fields morning and night, serving the whims of a master who had realized the potential for cheap, resurrected labor. She had helped him make his life, such as it was, become something other than what had been intended. And one day, he had promised, he would take care of her. When he had proven himself capable.

Everything she asked, every task she gave him, was a test. To see if he had what it took to become leader. Then, and only then, she'd said, would they expand the family. Such as it was.

Except that Adrien had grown impatient with waiting. With letting Marie make all the decisions. He was ready to lead the family—he knew it. Hadn't he proved it back in Boise? *He'd* been the one to sacrifice the others, to make that call.

But Marie kept telling him to wait. If he heard that word again, he would throttle her. The hunger in him for *more,* for another like him, for a companion who understood his loneliness, grew every day, became something he could no longer deny or keep quiet. And now he had finally met someone who intrigued him. Who made him, the creature who shouldn't desire . . .

Want. Crave. Need.

"Yes," Adrien said finally, watching as the girl exited a car and walked into the yellow house. The girl had a small, sad way about her, but Adrien intended to change that. All he needed was time. Not that he had a lot of time, what with Marie drooling impatiently beside him, but with this girl, he suspected he didn't need much. "You will like her. Very much."

"Is she healthy? That last one . . ." Marie shook her head. "She didn't last. We need a good one this time, Adrien. You must think with your head. You never do. *I'm* the one who does all the planning and the thinking. You just live off me like a leech."

Adrien bit back a retort. Now was not the time to argue. To remind Marie that if not for him, she would have gone back to the grave a long time ago.

The door shut, and the girl disappeared from his view. He sighed and turned away from the window. Patience, he told himself. Patience. "I am thinking. And planning."

Marie gripped his shoulders, forcing him to look at her. Even he, who had been among these people for nine decades, couldn't tolerate the sight of one who needed to be regenerated. The last woman's body they had taken hadn't been strong enough, young enough, healthy enough, to replenish Marie, and it showed.

In the skin peeling from Marie's body, her second one this century, in the fingernails that fell off with the slightest touch, scattering on the floor. In the labored breathing that heaved from her sunken chest, each exhale casting off the odor of rot. She was struggling to hold on to her remaining half life. Now she wanted a younger body.

Seemed such a waste to Adrien. Considering how badly Marie abused the bodies she had, Adrien would much rather have the girl for himself. To keep her by his side. To make her like him. But he'd promised Marie and he couldn't break his word.

Could he?

"I have very little time," she said, her words so strong and forceful in his face that he nearly tasted them. "You can't be wrong. Not again. Or I will—"

"She's the one." He jerked out of Marie's grip, hearing the nauseating soft clatter of yet another fingernail hitting the floor, and headed for the door. "It's nearly night. I need to hunt."

"Are you sure you're ready, Adrien? To hunt on your own?"

For years, they had done it in pairs. One circling the prey like a lion, the other pouncing. But now Marie was too weak. The past two times they'd gone out together, he'd ended up carrying her home. This time, Adrien would go alone.

Later, when they were strengthened by food, he would bring the girl by. Perhaps then Marie would be amenable to his idea. He cast one more glance at the yellow house.

From here, he could almost feel the girl's pain, the hole in her heart that had called to him that morning, drawing him like a light to her, of all the people in the school building. That hole was his way in, the chink in the wall that would eventually bring her from the yellow house—

To the cellar.

CHAPTER 6

Heather sat in the parked car and listened to her mother ramble on. And on. And on. God, why didn't she just go to work? Or the mall? They'd had this conversation, the I'm-concerned one, seven hundred times before.

"I think you should make an appointment with the psychiatrist, Heather," Mom was saying.

"Mom, I really have to get to school."

Her mother reached up a hand, as if she was going to touch Heather, but didn't. In the back seat, Meredith kept her head buried in her cell phone, texting away. Heather glared at her, wondering if she had told Mom what Heather had admitted at breakfast yesterday, if that was why she had to endure this talk. Again. Tweedledee and Tweedledum had been smart and walked to school. For some stupid reason, Heather had thought it'd be a good idea to catch a ride with her sister and mother, like ten minutes in the family Volvo would make everything normal again.

Right. Her life sucked. She lived with an aunt who hovered over her as if she might break any second, two cousins who defined *moron,* and a mother who didn't get it at all.

"Okay," her mother said finally. "Well, think about it. And have a good day."

"Good day? Yeah, I'll work on that." Suddenly, everything inside Heather's chest foamed and bubbled to the surface, like the time she'd mixed vinegar and baking soda in a test tube in Mr. Peachtree's class. Bubble, bubble, bubble, then *boom*—white foam all over the science lab table. "Mom, I gotta go."

Her mother started playing with the ends of Heather's hair, as if she were five or something. Last year, Heather might not have minded so much, but this wasn't last year, and the last thing Heather wanted right now was anyone in her face, telling her what to do or how to *make it all better.* It wasn't getting better and it never would.

Because every time she walked into that house and heard the floors and walls echo back, everything seeming so empty, so *dead,* she remembered. Her father was gone. Because she'd been an idiot and reached for her cell phone—and swerved into the opposite lane, straight into a tractor-trailer truck. God, she could still hear her father's scream. Her name drawn out in one last long word. She wanted to take it back, wanted to tell him she was sorry, so, so sorry.

That she should be the one in Parkwood Cemetery, not him.

"I know it's hard," her mother said. "But if you—"

"I gotta get to class," Heather said, the bubbling rising in her throat, threatening to explode in words she wouldn't be able to take back if she let them out. She pulled on the door handle and escaped from the Volvo, escaped from her mother, but most of all escaped from the memories that refused to go away. Her book bag tumbled onto the ground in her hurry to get out. She slammed the door before Mom could say anything else, then went to reach for the bag.

Another hand grabbed the strap before she could. She looked up—

Straight at Adrien. His dark sunglasses reflected back her surprise. "Oh . . . uh . . . hi."

Way to go, Heather. Could she have sounded any more stupid?

He smiled, slowly, and her stomach dropped as though she were on a roller coaster. "Hi, Heather."

He knows my name. Oh my God, he knows my name.

Adrien hauled up her book bag with one hand, as if it weighed nothing, and handed it to her. Their hands brushed when she took it, and Heather thought for sure she was going to die right there on the spot after touching for that half second.

"Do you want to walk in together?" he asked.

Walk in the building together? Heck, she'd walk to China with him. Adrien had to be the hottest guy she had ever seen. Half the girls in school were staring at them right now, undoubtedly wishing they were the ones who had dropped their bags. But they weren't. She was.

And Adrien St. Germain was looking at her, Heather Willis, waiting for an answer. Holy cow. Did he see her scar? Was he staring at the visible mark of her biggest mistake? If he was, he didn't say anything. Or seem at all repulsed. She let her hair fall forward, partially covering the line that sliced down her face.

"Heather?"

Oh, crap. She was just *standing* there. She nodded, then realized *mute* equaled *idiot,* and worked a whispered "yes" past her lips.

His smile expanded. "Great."

"Hey, Heather, how are you?" Mr. Edwards's tall, skinny frame draped a sliver of a shadow over her. She liked Mr. E. okay but right now wanted him to go away.

"Good."

"You planning on trying out?" he asked, waving at the sign tacked to the front door of the school, advertising the tryouts for *Romeo and Juliet,* the fall play.

"I don't know . . ."

"You loved acting," he said, his voice quiet, concerned. "It'd be a good way to get back to normal. Or start."

She wanted to scream that no one knew what normal would be for her, not again. But then she glanced at the poster, and she thought of how the stage lights would feel on her face, how her voice would echo in the empty auditorium during rehearsals, the rush she would feel on opening night. For the first time in forever, Heather thought about having fun. "Maybe," she said, still not ready to commit.

Mr. E. smiled. "Good." Then he walked off.

She'd expected Adrien to ditch her when he realized she was a drama geek, but he was still there by her side, patiently listening. He'd waited. She didn't care why.

Heather saw Sam standing to the side of the quad, joined by Meredith and some other yearbook people, watching them. She could tell from his face that her old boyfriend wasn't happy about what he was seeing. That he could read Heather's interest in Adrien as easily as a first grade book and that it had ticked him off. He watched for a long moment, and then he turned away and slipped into the building through a side door.

No wave hello. No smile. Nothing but a cold, hard look.

Heather shook it off. They were over—hadn't she made that clear? Sam had no right to be upset.

"Seems like you're having a difficult start to your morning," Adrien said.

Heather shrugged. "Just people trying to talk me into doing stuff I don't want to do."

"I can't believe anyone could talk you into anything," he said.

A thrill ran through her. This guy was interested in her? Was he for real? Or was she just seeing something that wasn't there? "Thanks," Heather managed, wishing she'd worn the blue V-neck A&F shirt today. She looked better in blue than black. Tomorrow, she'd definitely wear the blue.

"Is trying out for the school play so terrible?" Adrien asked.

Heather shrugged shyly. "I used to love drama. Maybe Mr. E. is right; maybe it would be good for me to get involved again."

Crap. She'd said too much. Now he'd start asking questions. Like why she'd stopped getting involved in stuff. What trauma had made her stop loving drama. Then she'd have to tell the whole story about how she'd killed her own father, by accident. She might as well wave goodbye to Adrien now. Like everyone else, he'd start backing up, creeped out by the chick who'd driven the family sedan into a Mack truck.

"You'd make a great Juliet," he said. Then he stopped and studied her for a long second, one that seemed to hold Heather's heart and breath hostage. She'd never felt this way before, not when anyone else had ever looked at her. "Maybe I should try out, too. Be your Romeo."

God, yes. Please, please, please.

"If you want to, uh, auditions are . . . are, um, after school on Thursday," she stammered. "In, um, the, um, auditorium."

God, she was such an idiot. She could barely talk.

He grinned at her, then glanced at his watch. "I gotta run. See you around, Heather."

"Okay." She watched him walk away, feeling like the world's biggest dork but, at the same time, exploding with a burst of happiness in her chest that was ten times stronger than the baking soda and vinegar.

Adrien St. Germain.

Was it possible to fall in love with someone she'd just met?

CHAPTER 7

The man had fought hard for his life. They'd toyed with him like a bug under a microscope, allowing him a window of hope, then closing it again. He'd hung in the cellar for a few days while they inhaled the scent of his desperation, letting it whet their appetite. Every so often, Marie or Adrien would go down there and take a tiny taste of the man, a finger, a toe, a strip of skin—an appetizer. Each time, the man's fear increased, his efforts to escape doubled. They laughed, watching his useless attempts to loosen the chains. For Adrien, this—this *game*—was the best part. Watching the prey go from confident and cocky to fearful and pitiful.

They'd broken him down a little at a time.

One bite at a time.

Now Adrien stood in the living room and chuckled at the man. His gray suit was no longer fine and pressed but tattered and bloody, his wide green eyes darting around the room, as if salvation lurked in the corners.

Nothing waited in those corners. Nothing but other hungry creatures, creatures who would clean up whatever scraps Adrien and Marie left behind.

The man lunged, taking advantage of his captor's momentary distraction, scrambling like a crab out of Adrien's grasp. "Let me go! Please!" He crawled toward the door, his legs shredded by their game, his fingers gone, his hands reduced to bloody stumps, and still, still he begged for his life. He had spirit, and Adrien had to admire that. In fact, it made the game all that much more fun to see how hard the man fought to survive. "I have a family! I—"

Adrien reached out and snatched the man back by the soft skin at the nape of his neck, his fingers sinking deep, deep, deep into his throat, until they emerged on the other side. The man's cries became gurgles, and his eyes widened until they seemed ready to pop. "Fighting us won't help," Adrien said, then smiled. "We need to eat. And you"—he laughed—"you are dinner."

The man pushed off from the floor and flipped, twisting Adrien's wrist. He flung out his arms and almost—*almost*—made Adrien let go. But Adrien was stronger, hungrier, needier. His fingers dug farther into the tender flesh of the man's neck until bones cracked, skin split. Blood spewed in an arc, followed by chunks of tissue.

The man opened his mouth to let out a soundless scream, but it was swallowed up by Marie, as she moved in and began to devour him while Adrien held the body for her. She shredded him with her teeth, her hands, as if he were a loaf of bread. Flesh, bone, and sinew littered the floor, painted the walls, soaked into the furniture.

Marie ate greedily, slurping, sucking, shoving bits of the man's body into her mouth. In minutes, he went from a human to a puddle of gore and entrails. In the shadows, the sexton beetles waited, appendages softly clicking on the wood floor. The blowflies hovered in a buzzing cloud, eyeing the decaying flesh. In minutes, the insects would do their work. All traces of the man would disappear. On the roof, the birds' claws clacked against the shingles. They would be disappointed because the kill had taken place inside and there wouldn't be anything left for them or for the hyenas. Later, Adrien would bring them something to reward their patience.

Either way, there would be no crime scene, not with their insect friends around to take care of the evidence and the ones in the tank to handle anything else. Being part of the walking dead had its advantages—like being surrounded by those who fed off the carcasses of the dead.

Adrien watched Marie make quick work of the man's body, hunger pulsing in his veins. In a few days, he would capture another and feed, too, but for now, he took pride in seeing Marie enjoying his handiwork. For so many years, she had taken care of him, and now, finally, he was proving himself to be man enough to return the favor.

Marie rose. Blood coated the front of her shirt, poured from her mouth in a slippery stream. A chunk of the man's brain clung to her upper lip. "For you," she said, and held out a gift. "For your first successful hunt alone."

In her hands, he saw the symbol of the passing of the torch, the exchange from one family member to another. What he'd waited ninety years for, tried so hard to live up to. And finally, finally, he had.

You have done good, boy. You have made me proud. You are ready.

He took the still-warm heart from Marie. "Thank you."

She nodded, once, then spun back to her meal.

Just before he consumed the man's lifeless heart, Adrien paused to look out the window. A light burned in the house next door. She was there.

Heather.

And soon, oh so soon, she would be here.

CHAPTER 8

The wind clawed at the windows, as if it were trying to climb inside. The shutters slammed against the outside of the house, angry, fast, Mother Nature's heavy-metal drummer. I got out of bed, my blanket around my shoulders, and crossed to the window. I unlatched the lock and lifted the bottom casement.

Rain and wind blasted in from outside, a hard slap across my face. I leaped back, sputtering and cursing. The storm swept into my room, knocking over a picture frame, whipping the blanket off my shoulders. Outside, the shutters seemed to double their beating of the siding.

I reached out for one of the shutters. The wood slipped past my hand the first time, but the second time, I caught it, brought it in, and latched it. The wind slammed harder, angrier.

Then, just as I began to reach for the second shutter, the wind stopped, as if it had been sucked into a giant vacuum. Everything went still, silent. I hesitated and listened.

Not a sound. Not a bird chirping. Not a car revving. Not a dog barking.

Nothing.

But how could that be? I mean, we didn't live in downtown Boston or anything, but there was always some kind of neighborhood noise. Someone driving by. A person talking too loudly on a cell. A teenager partying in his backyard. But *nothing?* Never.

Then, a slight whisper of a scent, something I didn't quite recognize at first, maybe because it was so unexpected. I leaned out the window into the black stillness. And inhaled.

Old Spice.

My father's cologne. Heather and I had bought him one every birthday, Father's Day, and Christmas—so many bottles, he could have opened an Old Spice store. And still, every time he'd opened one of those red boxes, he'd acted as if he'd just run out and ours was the best gift ever.

I leaned out farther, sure I'd see some old guy hobbling along, drowning in cologne.

No one.

Not even nosy Mrs. Cross—who was always up and spying on the neighborhood activities—sat out on her porch. Her house was silent and dark.

I ducked back inside and looked around my room, but I already knew I wouldn't find a cologne bottle here. After my father had died, I'd packed away most of the pictures, the sweatshirt of his I'd inherited somewhere along the way, and the baseball bat he'd given me for my sixth birthday. Shoved them into the closet.

Because I'd thought it would be easier to keep them there. Some days it was, some days . . .

It wasn't.

I'd left out only one photo, of Dad and me at a Red Sox game, taken six months before he died. I hated baseball, but he loved it, and he'd dragged us along to the games because we were the boys he'd never had. Now I missed the games. I'd go to a hundred if I could have him back.

Dad.

His scent wrapped around me as though he were there, and suddenly, I wanted him there, wanted what I couldn't have. I spun away from the window, searching for the photo. I saw it on the floor, the glass shattered, the picture dented. Anger rose in my chest, chased by the sharp pain of tears. I started to pick up the frame off the floor when the scent of

Old Spice came at me again, but this time in a massive burst, like someone had exploded a cologne grenade in my room. I circled around, trying to figure out where in the heck the smell was coming from.

Dad?

Impossible. But still, I looked. When I got to the window, I noticed the scent was ten times stronger outside. I braced my hands on the windowsill, squeezed past the space left by the single shutter that was still open, then closed my eyes—

And inhaled.

Dad.

God, it was as if he were standing right beside me, as if I could reach out and touch him. Then I opened my eyes and saw again an empty street.

No people.

No Dad.

A chill shivered through me, so bad that I wrapped my arms around myself to stop my body from shaking.

This was crazy. My father was dead. Not here. But for a second there, I really thought . . .

No. Impossible.

I drew back, about to close the other shutter, when I noticed something else. Heather was standing in the driveway. She was staring at the house next door. Not moving at all. Had she smelled the cologne, too?

The wind started up again, rustling leaves in the trees and blowing away the scent of the cologne so quickly and thoroughly I told myself I'd imagined it. Heather stood there a moment longer, then turned to go back into our house. I opened my mouth to call to her, then stopped.

Something glistened on her face. Tears.

Before I could say anything, she hurried inside. The closing of the back door seemed to echo.

I started to shut my window, and then I stopped. I heard a noise—like a soft *ch-ch-ch*—over and over again, coming from next door. The clouds shifted, and moonlight spilled over the St. Germain yard, illuminating it and revealing Adrien, in the backyard, burying what looked like a small suitcase or maybe a briefcase. Then the clouds shifted again and he straightened, and whatever he'd had in his hands was gone. He turned, looked up—

And stared straight at me.

I was up above him, enough to see just over the rim of his sunglasses. The streetlights cast a yellow glow over the alley that ran behind our houses and then onto half of Adrien's face. For one split second, I swore I saw what I had seen before in the classroom.

Death crawling in and out of his eye sockets. Long white worms, fat dark beetles, and a burst of flies buzzing around his head, as if he were roadkill.

Then he took a step back and disappeared into the shadows.

A scream roared up my throat, but I choked it back. I was crazy, I knew I was. Smelling Old Spice. Seeing worms in Adrien's eyes. I'd gotten my eyes checked yesterday, but shit, that doctor had clearly missed something. This was not normal.

The wind kicked up, and a gust of air whooshed the shutters closed, nearly slamming them on my nose. I shrieked, jumped back, and dived under the covers. It was a long, long time until I could close my eyes again.

CHAPTER 9

I was suffocating, wrapped in a blackness so deep, I couldn't see my own hands. I opened my mouth to call out, but no sounds came. Where was I? Beneath my bare feet, the floor was cold. Hard. Concrete. The air smelled damp and musty, almost sour. I heard a creaking, and I whirled around but couldn't see anything. I reached out, trying to touch something, anything that would tell me where I was. My fingertips brushed metal, and then I heard a clanging sound.

Chains?

I backed up, the concrete rough against my feet, and kept going until the backs of my knees collided with something hard. Wooden. I jumped away, then felt down, praying for stairs.

My fingers slid across the smooth wooden surface. Felt a lip, a corner. Another long edge. Not stairs at all. A box of some kind. I patted the top, both hands going around the wood edges now, trying to figure out dimensions. For some reason, it seemed ridiculously important to know what this was. My hand stuttered when a splinter sliced my palm but still I kept going. One edge, another, another, corners and angles, but my brain couldn't process a shape I couldn't see.

Then, finally, it added up. Two long sides. Two short sides. The top cut in a weird half hexagonal shape. A . . . coffin.

I jerked back, tried to scream, but again, there was no sound, nothing at all in the weird blackness except more dark. It seemed to consume me, suck me in, and swallow me whole. I had to get out of here. Even though I didn't know where I was, I knew it wasn't home. It was somewhere cold, musty, concrete . . .

A cellar?

Panic bubbled up in my chest, and I moved to the right, the left, but it seemed as if the darkness were crushing me, keeping me prisoner, and I couldn't escape. I heard a sound behind me, like a thousand teeth chomping. Something approaching. Footsteps.

I froze. Then something touched my arm, and I lurched forward, twisting at the same time, trying to get away, to escape the darkness, the monster attacking me—

I woke up. My blankets were twisted around me, covering my head. I flailed until I was loose, turned on my light, and sat up. My heart was still pounding.

That had been the darkness. A plaid bedspread. Not a cellar at all. Still, it had felt so real. I could still feel the wood of the coffin under my hands. *It had been a dream, nothing more,* I told myself. I sucked in a gulp of air, pressed a hand to my chest. Something painful pricked one of my fingers.

A splinter, long and thin.

And very, very real.

I ran into Heather on my way out of the bathroom, where I had spent fifteen minutes trying to extract the splinter.

"Took you long enough," she grumbled, and tried to push past me, but I stood in her way.

"So were you sleepwalking last night, or what?" I asked, even though I knew her eyes had been wide open. I hoped if she just acknowledged that the overwhelming scent of Dad had drawn her outside, I wouldn't feel as if I was losing it.

"I just went outside for some fresh air, that's all," Heather insisted, avoiding my eyes.

"Did you happen to see anything weird next door?"

"At Adrien's house? No." There was a defensive tone to her voice.

"I think I saw him burying something in the backyard."

Heather rolled her eyes. "I really doubt it, Mer. Now can I please get in the bathroom sometime this century?"

I gave up and retreated to the kitchen, where my mother sat at the table, flipping through a Pottery Barn catalog. Every so often, she'd get out her Sharpie and circle something we didn't need. Great. She'd moved on to mail-order shopping.

I could practically hear the folks at Visa sending up a collective cheer.

Aunt Evelyn was at the stove, making something that smelled delicious. Thank God someone in this house was still feeding us. Otherwise, I was pretty sure I'd have overdosed on microwaved burritos a long time ago. Tweedledee and Tweedledum were out in the driveway, shooting hoops. I half expected their heads to turn into basketballs, considering how much they played.

The Tweedle Twins would stop every couple of minutes and look next door. Their heads would get close together, as if they were conspiring against Adrien. His Camaro wasn't in the driveway, so their big plans were going to have to wait. Still, they looked pissed.

"Mom, what do you know about the people next door?" I asked.

She didn't look up. "Just regular people. Mother and son, I think."

"They keep to themselves, I've noticed," Aunt Evelyn said without turning around. "I haven't seen the woman leave at all. I don't trust people like that. Too quiet."

"Probably like their privacy," my mother said. "She might not know anyone in town yet."

Aunt Evelyn nodded. "Maybe. But still . . ." She stopped stirring the mystery meal and turned to face me. "Don't you think it's a little odd?"

"It's hotter than heck out. You'd think she'd want some air," I said. Our weather had been fierce the past couple of days. We'd had over-the-top heat that had yet to let up, making the weatherman look as though he'd hit the lottery every time he got on the air to announce some new record-breaking September temperature. "Come out and get a tan or something. They must be roasting in there. That house doesn't have AC, does it?"

My mother shook her head.

"Then why not open the windows? Put in a window air conditioner or something?"

Aunt Evelyn's tight gray curls bounced a little when she nodded in agreement. She was a wide, short woman, who had this thing for florals. Give her something with flowers on it and she'd wear it. Today it was a flowered dress that swooped out at the bottom, making her look like a bell-shaped rose garden. "I made muffins two days ago and brought them over, but they didn't so much as come to the door. That's not very neighborly, if you ask me."

My mother was still circling.

"Maybe they don't like muffins," I said.

Aunt Evelyn put a beefy fist on her hip. "Who doesn't like muffins?"

I thought a second. "You got me there, Aunt E."

"Exactly." She wagged a finger at me. "Plus . . ." Her lips puckered. "Those neighbors seem a little dirty."

"What do you mean?"

She lowered her voice and leaned in closer. "When I went over there with the muffins, I noticed they have bugs. Lots of them."

I raised a brow.

"I'm not talking about just a few flies on their trash, either," Aunt Evelyn went on. "They have swarms of flies that hang around their house. Not all the time, just part of the day. Then they're gone—whoosh."

"Maybe they just don't clean very well."

"They just moved in there," my mother said. "They probably haven't had a chance to call the exterminator yet."

"Maybe," my aunt said. "But there's just something odd about them. My boys have tried to make friends with that boy next door"—she said this as if they were all in kindergarten and the neighborhood were one big sandbox—"and he's been as cold as a dead mackerel. In fact, he's been mean to them. And I don't like people who are mean to my boys."

Proof in the pudding. The neighbors hated muffins and basketball. Start a witch hunt and run them out of suburbia today.

Except I had to agree. I hadn't even seen Adrien's mom yet, but I knew her son creeped me out. Had I really seen him in the yard, burying God knew what, for God knew what reason, in the middle of the night?

And then there'd been that too-real dream. I rubbed my thumb over the spot where I'd found the splinter. It was still red and sore, even though I'd tweezed out the piece of wood. I shivered. It couldn't be from the dream. I must have gotten the splinter from my nightstand. *It was just a dream,* I told myself.

Again.

Heather came into the kitchen. "What are you guys talking about?"

Aunt Evelyn beamed. My sister had joined in on a conversation, on purpose. I could see my aunt wanting to say something about that, but she didn't. "The new neighbors."

"Adrien? He's cool." She said it quietly, but her face lit up, as though she'd just found an extra Christmas present. I glanced over at my aunt. Her lips were pursed. She'd noticed, too.

"You like that boy?" Aunt Evelyn asked. My mother was still circling crap we didn't need, not even paying attention.

Heather shrugged. "He's all right."

She didn't fool anyone. You could have told she cared from ten states away.

"I'm glad you're getting out and making new friends," Aunt Evelyn said carefully, "but I just don't think this boy is a good one for you to hang around. He's . . . different."

"Way different," I dittoed.

Heather shot me a glare. "He's nice."

"I'm sorry, Heather, but I disagree," Aunt Evelyn said. "He's been outright rude to me. And to my boys. Ask Ted what he said yesterday when—"

Heather let out a shriek of frustration. "I swear to God, nobody in this house wants me to be happy. What is it? Is it easier to have Heather the Pity Case moping around? For once, I found someone who's nice to me, and all you do is bash him."

"We're not bashing him, Heather," Aunt Evelyn said. "I just think you should find . . . someone else. Sam, for instance, is—"

"I don't want Sam. I like Adrien. And you would, too, if you'd just give him a chance."

Aunt Evelyn's lips pursed again. "Mary, do you want to add something?"

Without looking up, my mother said, "Listen to Aunt Evelyn, Heather. She knows what she's talking about. If she thinks this boy is bad news, then I agree."

Heather let out a gust, then stomped out of the kitchen. Another unhappy customer in the Willis house. Aunt Evelyn sighed and went back to making breakfast.

I turned to my mother. I wanted to shake her, tell her to do *something,* to step up and be a parent. "Aren't you the one who rented the house to them?"

"Sort of," Mom said. "It was an easy transaction. Practically hands-off. They came in the office a little more than a week ago. Well, the son did. He said his mother was sick and took the rental package with him. They knew what they wanted, signed the papers that day, and had cash for first, last, and security. I didn't ask a lot of questions."

"Did you notice anything . . . weird about them?" I wanted my mother to jump up and say, *Aha, those are freaks I saw, signing on the dotted line. Let's kick them out of there now.*

But she'd already gone back to her catalog. "No. They took that eyesore off the market, and I made a commission. What more do I care?"

"We could have serial killers living next door, Mom. That's why you should care."

Aunt Evelyn hmm-hmmed agreement while she stirred.

My mother sighed. "Honestly, Meredith, you watch too many movies. I've met that boy. He seems nice enough, even if he hasn't been the most hospitable or neighborly since he moved in. And he seemed very worried about his mother. I'm sure he's a wonderful son." My mother circled a neon orange fish-shaped bowl. "They're just renters, Meredith. Don't worry so much."

"And Heather likes him. Aren't you worried about that?"

"Heather doesn't like him. She's just being dramatic." My mother drew a messy loop around the matching plates and serving platter. "You'll see. All of you are making a big deal over nothing. Nothing at all."

I shook my head and left the room. There was no talking to her, not while she was busy redecorating our house in Early Aquarium.

"So, did you finish that English essay yet?" Sam asked.

It was later that afternoon, and we were sitting at the diner, digesting our burgers. "That essay about the connection between love and violence in lit?" I shook my head. "Not yet. Writing it means reading the stuff Mrs. Allen gave us, and I'm trying not to improve my IQ this quarter."

Sam laughed, then dumped the third container of fries onto the paper-lined tray. One for each of us and a third to split, because we were both fry fiends. On my half, Sam sprinkled a crapload of salt, just the way I liked my serving of starch. I told myself that just because he remembered how I liked my fries didn't mean he thought of me as more than a friend.

"So . . ." he said, twirling a fry in some ketchup. "How are things at home?"

"Everything's cool," I said. Was he asking because he cared about me? Or he was just worried about my sister?

Sam held my gaze for a long while. "Okay. Well, if you ever need to talk about, you know, what happened with your dad, I'm here. Just call."

"Thanks." I wanted to ask if he'd be there if I called for no reason. Like, just because I missed him, wanted to see him. But I didn't.

"Nice sweater," Sam said. "I've never seen you wear it before."

He noticed what I wore? "It's new. A benefit of my mom's shopaholic trips."

"Too bad I can't get adopted into your family. I could use some new Nikes." He grinned.

"You used to be at our house often enough. You might already have been adopted."

"Except if I was, then I'd be your brother. And that would be weird."

"Yeah."

"And then you and I . . ." He dipped a fry, not looking at me. "Well, we'd probably fight over the remote." Now he looked up at me, and something inside me soared. "Or not."

"Definitely not."

"Good. Hey, Meredith, are you . . ." Sam started, then stopped. He twirled another fry in the paper tub of ketchup, then popped it into his mouth.

"What?"

"Nothing." He reached for another fry, picked it up, put it down again, then sighed and turned to face me. "I'm glad you're here, Meredith."

"You might change your mind when I finish off most of the fries." I laughed.

Sam touched my arm. When he did, a fire seemed to race through my veins. "I'm being serious. Heather thinks she's the only one who went through that accident, you know?"

I nodded.

"She forgets everyone around her worried, too. And when she stopped talking to me . . ." He ran a hand through his hair. "Well, it was tough."

"Yeah, I know what you mean." I knew, only too well. Heather had gone into a bubble and shut everyone out. Mom disappeared into the mall, and the rest of us had just been left to . . . deal.

"Anyway, that's worth a few fries." Sam grinned, and the serious moment lifted. "Want to order more?"

This time, his smile made butterflies race in my stomach. I worked up a smile in return, but it fell flat. "We, uh, gotta go. We have to get back to the yearbook office and finish processing those pictures I took the other day, or Mrs. Sawyer will be mad." I tossed our trash into the can, then followed Sam out to his car. "Thanks for paying for the burgers. I would have split it with you, you know."

"Not a problem. That's what friends are for, right?" He grinned again.

"Yeah," I said as we got into Sam's car. *Friends.* Just the word I wanted to hear right now. I'd thought we were moving in another direction, but I'd clearly been wrong.

He didn't start the car right away, just let his hand rest on the keys. "Because that's what we are, aren't we? Friends?"

I held my breath. "Are we?"

My cell phone started ringing just then, and I wanted to kill whoever had the bad timing to call me when I was waiting on what seemed like the most important answer in the world. I thought about not picking it up, but Sam stared at me with that "are you going to get that" look on his face, so I flipped it out. "What?"

"Well, what kind of greeting is that for your mother?"

"Sorry."

"I just wanted to tell you I won't be home until late to-night. I have an open house at seven at the new apartment building downtown."

"Okay." I figured that was it, but my mother talked to me for a few minutes more, just asking me the parental standards of how my day was going, whether I had any homework. Sam drove back to school and parked, and we got out before my mother finally stopped talking and said she'd see me late that night.

Sam and I headed for the yearbook room, powered up the computer, and sat down together to sift through a bunch of digital images. Since it was September, we were still mainly playing around with the stuff that would go in the yearbook. In a couple months, our advisor would start getting that pinched look on her face and remind us that we had to get serious or the yearbook would be filled with nothing but empty pages.

Outside the window, I could see the football team running drills on the field behind the cheerleading squad, throwing in a few extra grunts here and there, acting all mannish because the cheerleaders were practicing within visual distance. Every so often, one of the Bubble Bots—girls whose brains were solely focused on one goal: becoming prom queen before they graduated—would turn and send up a wave or a kiss toward one of the players. Twice, a running back tripped over his own cleats, more focused on his hormones and possibly hooking up than the ball.

I turned back to the computer. The pictures I'd taken over the past few days were just casual snaps as people were doing the end-of-the-day shuffle between lockers and parking lot. There were lots of goofy smiles and group hugs. "I like this one," I said, pointing to a pic of two senior girls making fish faces at the camera.

"Yeah, let's use that." Sam clicked on the image and dragged it over to the page we were working on. He went back to the group of pictures and started clicking again.

Adrien's image appeared on the screen. No smile, just him and his sunglasses. I didn't even remember taking the photo. Something bothered me about the picture but I couldn't put my finger on it. Sam hovered over it with the mouse, then dragged it to the trash bin.

"Don't like that one?" I asked.

"I think there are way better pictures in here." Sam clicked again, bringing up a photo of a group of kids hanging around a car that was all decked out in the school colors. "You're a great photographer, Mer."

"Thanks." I felt my face heat up. I realized then how close I was sitting to Sam. I put a little distance between us.

The door banged open and Cassidy came charging in, still flushed from cheer practice.

"Hey, Meredith, can I come over to your place?" she said.

"Sure. Did you want to study for the Spanish test or something?"

Cassidy snorted. "Since when do I study for anything? You know my motto. Minimum effort on stupid things. Like school."

I laughed. "Oh yeah."

Cassidy leaned in toward me and cupped a hand over her mouth so Sam wouldn't overhear. "I want to spy on Adrien."

"What? Why?"

"I gotta get the goods on him before anyone else does. Mer. I'm desperate. Will you help me?"

I started to say no, then stopped. Spying on Adrien could be a good thing. I was still a little freaked about what I thought I'd seen in his eyes, and there was that nagging feeling in my gut from the picture I'd taken. Maybe I'd feel better once I reassured myself I'd been seeing things. "Sure. Let's do it."

Cassidy hugged me so hard, I almost suffocated. "Oh, good!"

"Sam and I are about done here, and then we can walk back to my house," I said.

Cassidy sighed. "It's, like, a whole mile to your house. Geez. That'll take forever to walk. Do you think we could call a cab?"

I laughed. "Cass, you have to be the laziest cheerleader I've ever met."

She grinned. "I only cheer to date the football players. And because I like the skirts."

Sam closed out the yearbook software, then sat back in the chair and stretched. "I can drive you."

"You don't mind?" I said.

"Not at all," he said. He sent me a grin, and I wondered if he was giving me a ride only because it was a chance to see Heather.

We headed out to his car. Cassidy climbed in the back while I took shotgun. Sam sat in the driver's seat, and as he reached for the gearshift, his arm brushed mine. "Uh, sorry," he said, but he didn't move his arm. And I didn't move mine.

Oh, this was bad. Very bad.

"So," Cassidy said, shoving her face between us and making me beyond glad for Cass's in-your-face personality, "what do you know about the new guy, Sam?"

"That Adrien dude?" Sam shrugged. "The girls are fainting at his feet." He turned to me. "What do you think, Mer? If I wear sunglasses all the time, will I have the same effect on girls?"

"Totally." I grinned. Sam was in a good mood today, and I realized how much I had missed that smile. Those jokes. Maybe too much.

Cassidy let out a long-suffering sigh. "Boys. I swear, none of you are born with a single brain cell. I mean, what's Adrien like? Have you talked to him?"

"Yeah. He didn't say much. He's the quiet kind."

"But what did he SAY? Has he talked about any of the girls at school? Told you ANYTHING about where he's from? What he likes? WHO he likes?"

Sam glanced at her in his rearview mirror. "Cassidy, it's not like I sat down with the guy and had a heart-to-heart over the chicken fingers in the caf. You want info, ask him yourself."

Cassidy sighed, then slammed back against the seat. "You are NO HELP AT ALL."

Sam moved his hand on the gearshift, which made him touch me again. I didn't think he even knew he'd done it, because he didn't look at me or anything. "Sorry, Cassidy. I'll try harder to be a good spy."

"You will?" She perked forward again.

"No." He laughed. I bit my lip, then glanced at him, and the two of us shared a grin.

Like the old times when we were just friends and had jokes for the two of us. Except this time, his grin did something to me and I had to look away fast.

The ride to my house passed in a split second. Before I knew it, Sam had pulled into my driveway. "You think Heather's home?"

If anything told me where I stood with Sam—not that I should stand anywhere—that question did. He and I were on yearbook together, but that was as together as we were getting. I should have been glad. But for some reason, I wasn't.

"I don't know. You want to come in and see?"

He draped his hands over the steering wheel and stared at the house. "Nah. Just tell her I said hello. Maybe next time I'll come in."

"Okay. Sure." He had that beaten puppy look again. I wanted to hug him or something.

But I didn't.

Instead, I thanked him for the ride and got out of the car.

"Come on, come on." Cassidy dragged me toward the door. "We have to get inside."

"Why?"

"Because he's home," she whispered in my ear. Then she pointed next door, where the red Camaro sat in the driveway, baking in the sun. On the doorstep, Cassidy turned to me, with a devilish grin on her face. "So, Mer, do you own any binoculars?"

CHAPTER 10

We'd spent half an hour in my room, peering out the window with my father's old binoculars, and seen exactly nothing. The curtains next door were closed, and Adrien hadn't emerged from the house. Cassidy had done nothing but whine and eat almost all the chocolate chip cookies Aunt Evelyn had made us.

"We need to take this up a notch," Cassidy said.

"There's a notch above spying on the neighbors with binoculars?"

"Duh," she said. "You go up and look in the windows."

"Are you insane?"

She grinned. "Insane with lust."

"You girls sure you don't need anything else?" my aunt called from outside the door. "I can make brownies, too."

"We're fine, Aunt Evelyn."

"You *are* studying, right? Not just talking about boys?"

The way she said it made it sound as though we were in here giggling and writing "Mrs. St. Germain" all over our notebooks. Well, one of us wasn't. "Studying, Aunt Evelyn. I swear."

"Well, when you're done, I have more cookies in the kitchen."

"Thanks." We heard Aunt Evelyn walk away, then heard her footsteps going down the stairs.

"Nothing's happening next door and I can't see anything with these stupid binoculars. Let's go over there and peek in the windows, Mer." Cassidy pointed toward the St. Germain house. "Before it gets dark."

"What if we get caught?" I said. "You know they can call the cops for trespassing." That's all I needed right now—a stint in jail.

"If we get caught, I'll just smile and tell him I was lost." She posed, all flirty.

"Uh, yeah. I'd believe that. Not."

Cassidy swatted me. "I have a nice smile. Dr. Simpson tells me so."

"That's because your braces helped buy him a new Benz."

Cassidy sighed. "Listen, Mer, what else are we going to do to get information? I already tried all the other ways. I Googled him, I searched Facebook, MySpace. The guy is like a ghost. He's not online AT ALL. What kind of person has no online existence?"

"A real one?"

She rolled her eyes at me. "That's just not natural."

"It is if you have a life and you're too busy to be on the computer all the time."

"Like, who do we know like that?"

I didn't answer. She had me there.

She handed me the binoculars, and I moved to put them on my nightstand. They felt warm in my hands, and for a second, they made me think of my father. Of the Old Spice. It was as if he'd just been holding them and handed them off, like he used to at the Red Sox games. *Watch the pitcher, Meredith. If he's nervous, it'll show in his hands, his face. A good pitcher won't be affected by a few nerves. A bad one . . . can lose the whole game.*

"What are you doing, Meredith? LET'S GO." Cassidy practically ripped my arm out of its socket to haul me down the stairs. Aunt Evelyn was listening to some preacher on the radio and didn't hear us. We hurried out the front door, then circled around the side of the house to the garage. We stopped at the corner, then peered at the St. Germain house. Nothing moved.

I glanced across the street. Mrs. Cross's old Taurus wasn't in her driveway. Oh yeah, it was Thursday. Senior citizen discount day. She'd be gone most of the afternoon, scooping up her extra 15 percent off wherever she could. Good. That meant she wouldn't be toddling over to talk to my aunt and ask her why I was out playing spy commando in the backyard.

"Okay, Einstein, now what?" I asked Cassidy.

Cassidy started to speak, when there was a sound next door. Adrien stepped outside, got into the Camaro, started it up, and roared out of the driveway.

Cassidy sighed. "He's gone."

"That's good," I said. "Maybe now we can look inside the windows and not get caught."

"Maybe we'll see inside his bedroom," Cassidy said.

I shook my head. "You have a one-track mind."

She just grinned.

We looked around, didn't see or hear anyone else, then ducked down and scurried across the short expanse of lawn separating my house from Adrien's. Pressed ourselves to the peeling white siding of his house, then stopped again. Nothing.

There was a basement window at my feet and another window at shoulder level. I decided to try the higher one first. I signaled to Cassidy to be quiet, then slowly inched my head around.

The window was closed. Considering it was hotter than the surface of the sun outside today and the old house wasn't air-conditioned, I knew it had to be roasting inside that place. Not so much as a single box fan or window unit hung in any of the windows, either, at least none that I could see. Maybe the St. Germains were just that cheap. My uncle Larry was like that—he'd worn the same shoes since, like, 1972 and driven the same car since college. He reused his coffee grounds until the coffee came out Coppertone tan color and rinsed out his Ziploc bags so he could shove left-over grapes in them again and again.

Gross.

The curtains were parted only an inch or two, but enough to see inside. Still, at first I couldn't see anything because the house was dark and the window was dirty. I moved my head until I found a clear spot. I cupped my hand over my eyes to block out the sun's glare and pressed my face so close to the glass, my nose squished out a sweaty triangle.

"What do you see?" Cassidy asked, trying to get her own face in there, too. "I can't see anything. Geez, don't these people know about Windex?"

"I can't see much. It's dark in there. There's a sofa, a coffee table—"

"Boring," Cassidy said. "Tell me something cool. Something about *Adrien*."

She said his name as though he was a dream she'd been having. All long, slow, and sweet. I tried not to gag.

In the far right corner, I saw a blue glow. "Uh . . . he has a fish tank. More than one."

"Yawn, yawn. Something COOL, Mer."

But as I looked closer, my nose almost becoming one with the glass, I had to veto Cassidy's uncool vote. The tanks were long rectangles, twins in looks, but not in what they held. The first had big, flat silvery fish with bright red bellies, swimming in vicious, fast circles. The second tank had small fish, like the minnows I used to see at the edge of the lake where I went to summer camp. Hundreds and hundreds of them, darting up and down the tank.

Cassidy squeezed her face into the space beside mine. "Hey, I know what those are. We talked about them in science the other day. They're those people-eating fish. Purr . . . purr . . ."

"Piranhas?"

"Yeah, that's it. They're creepy. They eat, like, everything."

I looked again. I couldn't tell if those really were piranhas or not—my "fishology" wasn't good—but they sure looked like the fish I'd seen in movies where the people got sucked into unfortunate Amazon River endings. "If those are piranhas, then what are the other ones? Bait?"

Cassidy thought a second, her face screwing up as if she'd sucked down a watermelon seed. "Maybe Adrien's totally into creepy creatures. Maybe those are more eating fish."

I dropped down from the window and looked at Cassidy. "Small ones, like that? That eat people? I don't think there are any."

"Yeah, there are." Cassidy blew her bangs off her forehead. "Geez, Mer, you need to get out more. Don't you ever go to Chinatown?"

I shook my head. My father had always been the one who liked to drive into the city, and he'd taken me and Heather a lot, but his idea of a trip to Boston had meant Fenway Park or the Garden. Since he'd been gone, we hadn't been in to the city at all.

"My mom takes me there all the time. She says the green tea is healthier there." Cassidy rolled her eyes. "Whatever. I think she just likes to have an excuse to get away from my dad. He's like one giant stress ball."

Cassidy got quiet. I didn't know if it was because she was thinking about how grumpy her dad was, or that she'd mentioned her dad to the friend whose dad had been killed.

"So, ah, what's up with the little fish?" I asked.

Anything other than talk about people's fathers. Or lack of them.

"Oh, those. I've seen some just like them at this place my mom goes to for her pedicures. They put them—get this—in the foot tub. It is SO GROSS." Cassidy was back to talking in all caps. That meant she was back to her normal self. I liked that better than sad Cassidy, who dwelled on her parental issues.

"Why would they do that?"

"Oh, Mer, it's totally nasty. When I saw it, I wanted to HURL. The fish, they eat all the, like, dead skin off people's feet. Like pedicure cannibals."

Vomit churned in my stomach. "Those fish? The same ones?"

"I think so." Cassidy took a second peek. "They sure look the same."

"That's disgusting. Why would anyone want fish like that?"

"I dunno. Maybe Adrien's a closet manicurist?" Cassidy laughed.

"Or his mother. Maybe that's what she does for a living?" It was a possibility and explained the little fish—

But not the piranhas.

Who kept those kinds of fish in their house? Why? And what on earth would you feed them? I was thinking it wasn't a can of Tetra flakes.

I turned back to the window and tried to see anything else. But the house was pretty bare, as houses went. No photos on the tables. No clothes on the floor. Nothing much beyond the fish tanks and a few pieces of furniture. It was almost . . . sad. Maybe all their stuff was still in boxes, I told myself. But something told me that what I saw was all there was. "Well, he's neat. There's that."

"Always a bonus. My brother is a total pig. I hate that."

"Let's try another win—" I caught a movement out of the corner of my eye and dropped down as fast as a Navy SEAL. "Shit. I think there's someone in the house."

Cassidy slid down beside me, both of us flat on the grass. "Who? Adrien left."

"His mom, maybe?" I'd forgotten all about her in my big rush to gather information. "I don't know and I'm not going to go looking."

Cassidy frowned. "If we don't spy more, then how are we going to find out his secrets?"

She had a point. All we knew right now was that he collected weird fish. Wow. Way to go, Inspector Gadget.

I scooted a few inches forward, to the basement window. I figured whoever was upstairs probably wouldn't be going down into the cellar, so maybe we could get a peek in there.

"What are we going to see in the cellar?" Cassidy wrinkled her nose. "All people have in there are, like, spiders and stuff."

"True. But maybe we'll get lucky." Like the other window, the basement window was filthy and also covered by a curtain, except this one was black. One corner had fallen down, and I propped myself up on my elbows to peer inside. Because the cellar was dark, all I could make out were a few looming shadows. Oblong shapes—tall, skinny things . . . cabinets, maybe? A long row of rectangles beside those . . . maybe unpacked boxes? But no, that didn't seem right. They were oddly shaped. Like . . .

Coffins.

Impossible. I leaned in closer and saw something hanging from the ceiling—actually, *two* somethings. Long and thin, and I tried to wrap my mind around what they could be. They were hidden by the shadows and I couldn't figure it out.

I mean, it was a basement. People had all kinds of weird things in their basements. Mostly junk. Why should a couple of hanging things bother me?

Cassidy tapped my shoulder. "Come on, Mer, let's go around the other side and see if one of the windows is Adrien's bedroom."

Suddenly, the hairs on the back of my neck stood up. Someone was there, I knew it. Had they seen us spying? I looked around, but I didn't see anyone or hear the roar of Adrien's Camaro. Still, nerves fluttered in my gut. "I think we're pressing our luck. We should go back."

There was a crash inside the house, the sound of glass breaking, and both of us jumped. "Yeah, you're right," Cassidy said quickly, and we both broke into a run, heading for my garage. I didn't notice until I stopped how fast my heart was racing.

Cassidy let out a sigh. "Nothing. Waste of time."

"Yeah," I said, except I had a feeling I'd learned something. I just didn't know what.

"Maybe we can do this again some other day. Find out more about Adrien then, or at least see him doing SOMETHING, ANYTHING. Anyway, I'll catch you at school tomorrow." Cassidy headed down my driveway, sending a wave over her shoulder. Seconds later, she was gone, disappearing around the corner of my house and heading toward her own, two blocks away.

I was almost to the back door when I got the creepy raise-the-hairs-on-the-back-of-my-neck feeling again.

I stopped walking. Told myself I should turn around.

A chill ran down my spine. Something or someone was behind me. I knew it.

I should turn around.

But that internal sixth sense—the one that told you not to talk to the creepy guy working the counter at the sub shop—kicked in and blared one message:

Don't look.

Don't do it.

Don't, don't, don—

Quickly, I turned.

Nothing. No one. The yard was as empty as it had been five minutes ago.

But the hairs on the back of my neck totally disagreed. A blast of goose bumps dittoed.

I spun to the left. The right. Then back toward the house again. Just as I finished my one-eighty, I saw a flash of white next door. The black curtain that had been in the basement window a second earlier was now gone and that meant—

Something—or someone—was in the cellar. Watching me.

And what was worse, I had a feeling he or she or *it* knew that I'd just been there. Watching them.

CHAPTER 11

Heather stood on the scarred wooden stage, feeling like the world's biggest idiot. Why had she agreed to try out for this stupid play? Mr. Edwards had handed her Juliet's lines and was making her stand there while every bad actor loser in school slobbered out Romeo's.

"I would I were thy bird," Wendell Marks said, his voice cracking on the last words.

"Sweet, so would I," Heather replied with all the enthusiasm of a sleepwalker.

Wendell took two stumbling steps forward, as if he was going to kiss her or something. Heather moved to the right and shot Mr. Edwards a look of annoyance. "Mr. E.!"

"Heather, this is called acting. That's why you have to act." He waved his hands in a circle. "Emote. Be Juliet."

Heather looked back at Wendell and wrinkled her nose.

"I would if I had a Romeo who didn't make me want to barf," she muttered.

"Pretend Wendell is your true love." Mr. Edwards shoved his glasses up on his nose and blinked behind them, his eyes wide and owl-like. "You can do this, Heather. I know you can."

Yeah, that was what everyone said. Except lately, Heather hadn't been feeling as though she could do anything. Last night, she couldn't sleep and had the crazy idea of going to Adrien's house to pay him a late-night visit. Then, out of nowhere she'd smelled her father's cologne, and it stopped her in her tracks. It had been like a cruel gift. She'd wanted so badly to see her father—to apologize, to make up for what she had done. Yet at the same time the scent had been a searing reminder of all that had happened, almost too painful to bear.

She wanted to go home now. She didn't even want to be in this stupid play.

"Mr. E.," Heather began, "I don't think I want to—"

"Do I get to kiss her?" Wendell flipped a few pages. "There's a kiss in here, right?"

Nausea rolled in Heather's stomach. "Mr. E., there's no way—"

"Are you still holding auditions for Romeo?"

The voice came from the back of the auditorium, from

the darkest shadows, but Heather recognized it immediately. He sounded like a latte, rich and bad for her, but oh so delicious.

Adrien. He was here.

Mr. Edwards pivoted, cupping a hand over his eyes. "Technically, yes. And you are?"

"Adrien St. Germain."

Mr. Edwards made a note on his clipboard. "Okay, Adrien. And you think you'd make a good Romeo, do you? Well, go on, let's see what you've got for us."

Adrien took his time striding down the crimson carpet of the auditorium, as if he were the director, not Mr. Edwards. Beside Heather, Wendell let out a whine and something about how he already had the part, but Heather ignored him.

Adrien took the stairs two at a time. When he hit the stage, he seemed to take over the space, becoming so much larger than the twenty-by-thirty-foot area. He stopped in front of Heather. The room hushed. Even Wendell backed up two steps and stopped talking midwhine.

"Let me get you a playbook, Adrien," Mr. Edwards said.

"No need, sir. I know the lines." Adrien's gaze had locked on Heather's.

She forgot to breathe. Forgot to do anything but stare back.

"Suit yourself," Mr. Edwards said. "Action."

Adrien reached out a hand and took Heather's in his own. Her heart stopped, and a zing of electricity ran through her. He was touching her, honest to goodness touching her. Whether for the play or not, she didn't care. She was going to memorize this moment.

For just a second, it was as if she could read Adrien's mind. Could hear him whisper to her. *You are my Juliet. You, Heather, and only you.*

"'If I profane with my unworthiest hand This holy shrine'" Adrien said, his sunglasses-hidden gaze never leaving Heather's, "'the gentle sin is this: My lips, two blushing pilgrims, ready stand To smooth that rough touch with a tender kiss.'"

The entire auditorium seemed to have disappeared. She didn't notice the sophomore art class painting sets in the back. Didn't notice Wendell sulking in the corner. Forgot about Mr. Edwards sitting in the orchestra pit with his notepad and pen. A smile rolled over her face and she did a half curtsy, the kind she imagined a woman in Juliet's day might do. "'Good pilgrim, you do wrong your hand too much, Which mannerly devotion shows in this; For saints have hands that pilgrims' hands do touch, And palm to palm is holy palmers' kiss.'"

Adrien shifted closer—or was that Heather's imagination?—and his head dipped slightly as his voice deepened. "'Have not saints lips, and holy palmers too?'"

The next line . . . what was it? She'd read the play a thousand times and knew it by heart because it was her favorite of all the Shakespearean dramas, but for the life of her, she couldn't remember what to say now. She opened her mouth, and nothing came out.

A slight smile danced on his face. He skipped to Romeo's next line, covering for her. "'O, then, dear saint, let lips do what hands do! They pray; grant thou, lest faith turn to despair.'"

And then he moved forward, closing the gap. In her head, she heard him—or heard her imagination. *You are so beautiful. Everything I've always desired.*

Oh, God. Heather caught her breath, sure, so sure, he was about to kiss her. Even though her memory had become a foggy mess right now, she was pretty sure this was not the scene where Romeo was supposed to kiss Juliet, but she didn't care. She just wanted—

"Bravo, Adrien. Bravo!" Mr. Edwards shouted, then started clapping.

Adrien stepped back, releasing Heather before turning toward Mr. E. "Thank you, sir."

"And Heather, that's exactly the kind of emotion I wanted to see! You came alive in that scene!" Mr. Edwards threw up his hands, as if he'd just won the lottery. "I think we have our Romeo and Juliet!"

"But, Mr. E., I thought I was going to be Romeo," Wendell said. "I studied the lines and everything."

Mr. E. glanced at the skinny, freckled redheaded kid. "How about you be Adrien's understudy? If he's sick or unable to play Romeo for whatever reason, you can take his place."

Wendell clapped his playbook to his chest. "I'll be the best understudy *ever*, Mr. E. You won't be disappointed."

Heather would be, should she have to act across from Wendell. Ugh. She'd rather have the flu for a year than kiss Wendell. She prayed Adrien never missed a day of practice.

She glanced over at him and wondered if he was as excited as she was. She couldn't read anything behind his sunglasses. What was up with those, anyway? Did he ever take them off? She wondered what color his eyes were. Blue? Brown? Blue, she decided. Deep ocean blue.

Either way, sunglasses or not, she could feel something. In the way he stood, not too close, but not too far away from her. In the way he had seemed to stare at her, even if she couldn't see his eyes exactly. She could feel . . .

A simmering between them.

She stood on the stage, paired with Adrien in a fictitious play, and wondered if the impossible could happen. That this totally hot Romeo could fall for this ridiculously ordinary, slightly damaged Juliet.

CHAPTER 12

The night's hunt took Adrien far more time than he would have liked. Every hour he spent stalking the streets was another hour he risked exposure. The hyenas skulked far behind, keeping to the shadows. But he could hear their heavy panting, their frantic pawing, as they circled and paced, waiting for any morsel they could get.

Adrien had found—and rejected—several human specimens. They were too young, too old, too visible. The conditions had to be just right, or he'd be caught. Plus, he needed prey that would sustain him for the days ahead. Why bother with a decrepit human, when it would barely sate his appetite? He'd simply have to hunt again, even sooner. Better to do it right the first time. And so he ventured farther and farther from the center of the town, his hunger growing until it thundered in his head, blinding him to everything but the need to eat. *Eat, eat, eat.*

While he hunted, he calculated his options with the other girl. Meredith. She was a problem. She thought he didn't know about her little spying trip this afternoon. Fool. Did she think he didn't have spies of his own? Ones more than happy to report to him, to protect their own interests?

The animals had been the ones to communicate the threat to Adrien. Marie, however, had kept silent. She had to have seen her—Marie never left the house anymore. The question was why she had kept it secret. That bothered him. Gave him yet another reason to mistrust her. The more she decayed, the more mistakes she made. The more he saw the wisdom in eliminating her.

If Marie didn't get him killed first. She'd been the one to grab those two boys in Panama, then, in Boise, two women, in broad daylight at that. She'd been impatient, ruled by hunger. As soon as the humans were in her possession, Marie had started to eat. Didn't even wait to get to someplace safe, private. The others had joined in, and then someone had seen them—and her mistake had nearly cost them everything. That's how she operated. On hunger, not on brains.

Adrien had learned to control his needs. To put the family—such as it was—ahead of everything else. Marie had not. That was why he was done with her. She was an albatross, plain and simple. One he needed no more.

He also needed to eliminate Meredith. But her disappearance would be noticed and interfere with his plan to take Heather. He needed another way to rid himself of the Meredith problem. In any other city, he'd simply have taken Meredith back to the cellar and devoured her. But there was something about Meredith. Something different. She wasn't falling for his spells like the other girls.

Long ago, he'd learned powerful tricks from the Haitian witches. Developed ways of touching people and connecting with their minds, reaching into their deepest desires and using those to his advantage. For nine decades, those tricks had worked whenever he'd needed them to. Until now. Until Meredith. Why?

Perhaps he just needed to try harder. Perhaps he'd been distracted by the scent, the sight, of her sister, so close by. Yes, he decided, that was it. Still, an uneasiness rolled through him and whispered doubts about that logic.

For now, he'd worry about eating. After that, he'd have a clearer head. Their last meal had been mostly Marie's. She'd devoured the man's flesh, his organs, leaving the scraps for the bugs. They'd let the piranhas clean the bones, then buried the bones inside the man's briefcase in the backyard. The meal had been enough to recharge Marie, but not enough to restore her body. For that, she needed to pour her soul into another, a far more complicated and dangerous venture.

Adrien was the stronger one, the younger one, and he could afford to wait to eat. Marie, however, was falling apart—literally—and was now dependent on him.

How ironic. The roles had reversed. The only thing she possessed was the Knowledge. The key to taking Heather and making her into one of them.

When they'd arrived here, in small-town America, where nothing bad ever happened to anyone, the deal had been simple. Adrien would seek out a life form that Marie could take over, a young girl she could become, allowing her to shed the body that was nearly as useless to her as air to breathe. He'd intended to do just that, to keep their agreement. To do what Marie asked, because he owed her that much for helping him after he had been raised from the dead.

For so long, Adrien had felt as if he had a debt to pay her. And pay he had. All these years, Adrien had served Marie. Been loyal and steadfast and had waited. Waited for her to share the information handed to her by the others like them. But she hadn't.

Boise had been the turning point for him. The moment when Adrien had realized that he'd either learn to take control—

Or end up like the other two.

One thing about beings like himself and Marie: Loyalty ran about as deep as their bloodless veins. One day—and that day always came eventually—the ones with the Knowledge turned on the ones who'd been raised for one purpose only. To serve.

Adrien had served enough. It was time to become one of the ones with the Knowledge. A new hunger rose inside him, one more powerful than the one for human flesh and organs. A hunger for power, for a life of his own. One not under another's thumb. In that new life, he saw himself—

And her. *Heather.*

That sweet, sweet girl. His—not as a meal, but as a partner. Someone to walk beside him in this empty, eternal existence. He licked his lips and clenched his fist, picturing her peach-soft skin and wide brown eyes. Soon, oh so soon, she would be his. Together, they would hunt and devour the weak. Their power would reach levels Marie had never even dared to dream.

But Adrien had. Oh, Adrien had.

A pounding urge roared inside him, like a ticking time bomb. He pushed it down, put it aside, because for now, he had to concentrate on finding just the right prey. Then, after he devoured the flesh and organs, he'd savor the brain. Eat each lobe with care. For the brain held all the information and the soul—the keys Adrien had used and cultivated to make him fit in, make him look, sound, and act like one of *them.*

He had learned to savor the brain, to eat it slowly, with reverence. Marie—

Well, she never had. That was just one of the differences between them. And why he would be the victor in this death versus the dead battle.

He skirted an abandoned building. The brick exterior had begun to crumble, falling at his feet and crushing to powder beneath his boots. Rats skittered in and out of the building's crevices, not even pausing to acknowledge Adrien's presence. Just one more night creature among dozens of others. He heard the hyenas move in, taking up stations in the open doorways. They sat on their haunches, patient. The moon hung low and large in the sky, casting a white glow over the street. Adrien paused, sniffing the air. There was someone here. Someone . . .

Worthy of his appetite.

He heard the female voice approach, caught the sour scent of alcohol on her breath. She was singing, probably along with one of those silly wired things people stuck into their ears to listen to loud, obnoxious music. Adrien ducked into the building. The rats and hyenas fanned out, away from Adrien, as if they wanted no part of what he was about to do. That was fine.

They could have the leftovers.

Footsteps, then the soft, sweet scent of living flesh. Adrien sprung from his hiding place and attacked, digging his fingers deep into his victim's throat. The slim silver radio clattered to the ground, still playing its tinny, muted tunes that no one would ever hear again. The voice stopped, the blood began to flow—

And at last, Adrien's hunger was quenched.

CHAPTER 13

What are *you* doing here?" Heather looked at me as though I'd walked into her room to rob it. She turned to her closet and began hanging up the clean clothes that were piled in a mountain. Just for something to do to avoid talking to me, I was sure, because Heather would rather run a marathon than clean her room.

I plopped onto her unmade bed. After the weirdness last night with the Old Spice, I was in no mood to go to bed. And I knew Heather had experienced it, too. Maybe if I talked to her, really talked to her about the hard stuff, I could find that bridge we'd lost six months ago. Lord knew I had to do something, because I felt sometimes as if I was losing Heather, too, and I just . . . couldn't do that. I wasn't sure how to begin, so I just said, "I miss him."

She paused, a long-sleeved pink shirt halfway to the hanger. Didn't say anything.

"I miss his jokes," I said. "They were stupid and corny, but they were Dad's. Remember?"

She nodded. It was something.

"And the way he tried to convince Mom we should have dessert first and dinner second."

She put down the shirt. "Remember the time we had cake for breakfast?"

Heather had barely talked about Dad since he'd died. This was a huge moment, and I knew it. So I held my breath and just nodded.

"After that, he made it a rule that we had cake for breakfast on our birthday. Every year."

"I remember that," I said. "Mom about died, but I think she always ate the biggest piece."

A smile flickered on Heather's face, then disappeared, like a TV losing power. "We didn't do that on my birthday."

Oh, crap. We hadn't. I'd thought of suggesting it—I remembered having the thought the day before Heather's birthday a few weeks back in August, but then I'd taken one look at Heather's face, all gray and sad, and thought maybe a reminder of our father wasn't such a good idea. What if I had asked Mom to buy a cake for breakfast? Would we be where we were right now?

"I thought about doing it," I said. "I just didn't want to . . . make you more sad."

"That's okay."

"Tell you what—next time, we'll get two cakes. One for me, and one for you. And we'll stay up all night and watch movies. Just like we used to with Dad when we were little."

Heather laughed. Not a big laugh, but still, a laugh. Another step forward. "We never made it all night, Mer. We'd always say we were going to stay up until the sun came up and then we'd both fall asleep before the first movie ended."

I grinned. "I think that was part of Dad's plan. I don't think he wanted to stay up all night, either. But the camping in the living room part was fun."

"Yeah," Heather said, and she smiled at the memory. "It was."

I felt as though I had an in with her now, as if a door had been opened, and maybe it was time to talk to her. We weren't fighting, and maybe if I tried a soft approach, rather than hammering on her like I had before, I could find out what was really going on in her head these days. "So, Heather, what's up with you and Adrien?"

A hardness came over her face, and I knew I'd started wrong. But there was no going back now. I was stuck with the bad approach and had to try to land this plane without crashing. "He seems like a nice guy and all"—somewhere I had read that starting with a compliment was always a good idea—"but . . . don't you miss Sam?"

"Sam and I are over, Meredith."

Okay. I mean, that was good. I still hadn't told her I liked Sam and wasn't sure if I should. The last thing I wanted was for Heather to get hurt again—which was why her infatuation with Adrien had me so concerned. "Do you think maybe Adrien could be, like, a player or something? I mean, every girl in school is practically drooling at his feet."

Her face flushed. "If other girls like him, it's because he's being nice."

"I'm just saying, Heather. That's all."

She threw up her hands, crossed to the window, and stared out at the darkness. "Why don't you want me to be happy?"

"I do, Heather. Really."

"Well, Adrien makes me happy. In fact . . ." She let out a long breath. "I think I might be falling in love with him."

That sentence hung in the air between us for a long, long time. And filled me with fear.

Falling in love with him.

Adrien stood frozen to the spot beneath Heather's window, replaying the words she'd spoken. It was what he had wanted. What he had dreamed of ever since he'd first seen her.

With the back of his hand, Adrien swiped the last remains of his meal from his face, licking off the few bits of brain matter on his skin. Already, he could feel the regenerating power of the young woman he had devoured. The other human's blood, organs, and, most of all, her brain pulsing through Adrien's walking corpse body.

The dead woman's thoughts, still warm, ran through him, giving him a window into the female heart. Why did Marie refuse to be patient enough to learn this? Such power could be amassed, simply by taking the human's thoughts, too. This was how he had learned to manipulate, to control, those around him. Tap into their brains and whisper exactly what they want to hear.

Females were far more receptive to him than males. Females let him get closer, left more windows open to their soul. They were, simply put, more vulnerable. Silly, pathetic humans.

He chuckled. What better way to woo Heather than to literally consume the deepest thoughts of the female brain, then use them on her? Someday, when she was like him, she would love the story of how he had killed this woman, using her brain to bring Heather closer.

He waited beneath the window of the yellow house until he heard the sister—Meredith, that problem he had yet to erase—leave. Everything stilled around him. The night birds stopped calling, the breeze stopped blowing, the crickets stopped chirping. He looked up at the window—her window—and whispered a single word.

"Heather."

A moment passed, and then, just as he'd known she would, Heather appeared at the window. She'd heard him, not just because he'd spoken her name, but because they shared a connection, one that grew every time he touched her. Her wide brown eyes softened when she looked down at him, and the hunger grew stronger in Adrien.

God, how he wanted her. To have her share in this painful, never-ending, lonely eternity he had been walking for so long that he'd stopped tracking the time.

"Adrien." His name slipped from her lips in a whisper. "What are you doing here?"

"I wanted to see you."

She smiled. "You did?"

To his right, a small shed butted up against the house. Adrien swung his body up and onto it, which brought him just a couple feet below her window. If he'd wanted to, he could have climbed inside her room with little effort. But no, not now. That would be too forward. He could still hear the prey's memories—*that crazy boyfriend practically stalked me*—and that made him hang back. Move carefully. Slowly.

The last thing he wanted to do was scare his precious Heather, make her think he was some "crazy boyfriend."

"In school, there are so many people around," he said. "It's hard to talk."

"It is."

"And I really like talking to you."

The smile on her face widened, and he sensed that chasm in her soul opening to him. She was perfect, this vulnerable, wounded bird, who so clearly needed someone—someone like him—to show him how wonderful life could be if only she had forever on her side.

"Today, at the audition, your performance was wonderful," he said. He no longer remembered how he had wooed women when he had been something other than what he was today, but he could hear the thoughts of those he had consumed. *Wanna make me happy? Compliment me once in a while,* the women said in a common refrain.

Heather smiled, and a faint redness filled her cheeks. "Thank you."

"It seemed so real. As if we . . ." He paused a moment, letting her think he was searching for the words. "As if we really were Romeo and Juliet."

A happy sigh escaped her. "Well, yeah, but we were acting."

"Maybe *you* were. But I . . . I wasn't. It was real for me."
He wanted to tell her how much he related to Romeo. A
man misunderstood simply because of who he was, in love
with a woman he shouldn't be. A woman with a family who
despised him, who protested their union. And he, a man
willing to go to the extreme—death—to have her.

Soon, he told himself, flexing his fists at his side, soon he
would. Patience.

Her mouth opened, but she didn't speak. He knew then
he had her. She was falling for him, as he had hoped. He felt
his heart—whatever he still had that passed for a heart—
quicken, and his desire to have her now, not a day from now
or a week from now, multiplied tenfold.

"I want to be with you, Heather," Adrien said. "I want to
see you."

"I . . . I . . ." She blinked. "You do?"

"Will you be . . ." He rose onto his toes and reached for
her hand, waiting for her to look into his face. He left the
sunglasses on, saving that pièce de résistance for the end,
when he'd show her the truth of who he was. If he showed
her now, she would be afraid, and he didn't want to scare her.
Later, she would be ready to see the sweet beauty of resurrected death.

"Be what?"

"My Juliet?" he asked, giving her delicate fingers a squeeze. Her skin was so soft and smelled like peaches. Delicious, sweet. Wonderful.

Be mine, he whispered through their mental connection. *Be mine always. I never want to let you go.*

"Oh . . . my." A bigger smile burst across her face, and she nodded. "Yes, Adrien. I will."

Joy rose inside him. He would no longer be alone. Heather would be his.

Forever.

"Heather? Are you still up?"

From another room came the voice of the old woman who lived in the yellow house. Adrien cursed and dropped Heather's hand, then ducked out of view.

"Just, um, having trouble sleeping, Aunt Evelyn," Heather called back.

Aunt Evelyn. That's who she was. That nosy witch who had come by with the food the other day. He'd been half tempted to eat her but had been smart and ignored her instead. She was the mother of those idiots who kept trying to talk to him at school. The ones who seemed determined to distract him from his sole goal—

Heather.

"I thought I heard voices."

The aunt's voice was closer now. In Heather's room. Adrien crouched down farther, cursing the woman's timing.

"No, that was just my radio," Heather said. She shut the window, and the sounds of conversation were muffled.

Adrien dropped down off the shed, took one last look at the yellow house, and returned to his own.

Aunt Evelyn. He would deal with her. Oh, he would deal with her. In a way that would ensure she would stop interfering with his plans.

CHAPTER 14

When I got up the next morning, Heather was gone. Just a blank space by the door where her Lands' End backpack usually squatted. No Keds in the closet, no bowl in the sink.

"She left," Aunt Evelyn said, as she shuffled into the kitchen in her fuzzy pink slippers. Her bed-head hair stuck out in twenty different directions. "Didn't want any breakfast or anything. And I even offered to make French toast."

Heather's favorite. She'd skipped that to head to school? Something was up.

"Where's my mom?"

"Work." She made a face. "Again."

I shook my head and headed for the cabinet to make the all-important morning decision—cereal or junk. I grabbed a Pop-Tart—much to Aunt Evelyn's nutritional horror—then fished enough quarters out of the change jar to pay for lunch and headed out the door. The Tweedle Twins were standing in the backyard, glaring at the house next door. "He's a chickenshit," Tweedledee said.

"Who?" I asked.

"Adrien. Left already. Probably saw us coming and took off."

"Yeah," Tweedledum said.

"Yeah," Tweedledee agreed.

"Did you ever think he might just have wanted to get to school like the rest of us?"

Tweedledee snorted. "He's running scared. We told him to meet us here this morning. Told him we had 'business' to discuss."

"Yeah, business," Tweedledum echoed with a little laugh.

"What is it with you two and him? You sound like a rerun of *The Sopranos*. All because he didn't want to be on the basketball team?"

"More than that, cuz. He stole my girlfriend."

"Mine, too."

I'd wondered if he was some kind of jerk, just out to score. "He stole both of your girlfriends?"

My cousin snorted. "Try every girl in school, because they all like him. They follow him like sheep. It's like he's got this spell over them. Renee won't talk to me. I asked her to homecoming, and she ignored me. Asked her to the movies—nothing. It's like I'm not even there. The only thing she talks about is Adrien this, Adrien that." Tweedledee spat on the ground, and though he had macho written all over his face, I could see the hurt in his eyes. "I swear to God, I hear his name one more time, I'm going to explode."

"It'll pass," I said. "He's the shiny new toy."

"Oh, it'll pass all right," Tweedledum said. "Because we're going to *make* it pass."

Tweedledee nodded. "I went up to Adrien after school yesterday and told him if he didn't lay off talking to my girlfriend, I was going to pummel him. He acted like it was no big deal. Told me she was free to like who she wanted, and if I wasn't human enough to keep her, that was my problem." He threw up his hands. "What the hell is that supposed to mean?"

I told him I didn't know.

"So we got up early to pummel him *before* school." Tweedledee grinned. "See if Renee finds him so interesting with a bloody nose."

"Yeah, except he's gone already," Tweedledum scoffed. "Chicken."

"Chicken," Tweedledee agreed.

Unease settled in my stomach. Something told me Adrien had left early not to avoid a fight with my cousins, but for another reason. "Heather's gone, too," I said.

"You think he's got her with him?" Tweedledee cursed.

"That's the last straw. Let's go," he said to Tweedledum. "We'll catch up to him before school."

The two of them broke into a run, their paces matched in some kind of twin physical energy. They were gone in a burst of speed, hauling butt for school. I started after them—a lot slower, considering how much I hated athletics and gym class.

Before I left my driveway, I glanced back at the St. Germain house. All was quiet and still. No movement behind the closed windows. No lights on, no car in the driveway. Still, that eerie feeling crept up my neck again. I took a couple steps toward the older house, curiosity dragging me forward as if I were on a rope. I wanted to know more, not just what my cousins had told me, but answers to all the other weirdness that was behind those doors.

What were those fish about? What had been in that cellar? What on earth had Adrien been burying the other night? And what about the cologne I'd smelled? The dream I'd had? The weird way Adrien stared at me? Taken individually, none of it was anything. But all together . . .

"Meredith Willis!"

I jumped. Spun to the right and looked across the street, my hand over my chest to stop my heart from beating out of control. "Mrs. Cross. You scared the crap out of me."

The old woman made a face at the word, then leaned forward in her rocker. Her horizontal-striped housedress flowed around her like a cloud, and she still had her hair in curlers, tucked under a clear vinyl shower cap. I wondered why she bothered—except for the grocery store, Mrs. Cross hardly went anywhere and had fewer visitors than a prisoner on death row. "What are you doing over there?"

"Nothing, Mrs. Cross." But the words came out in a guilty mumble all the same.

She harrumphed. "You seen those new neighbors yet?"

I nodded.

"You like them?" She didn't wait for an answer. "I don't. They don't even have time to say a howdy-do. I say hello, they say nothing. What kind of rudeness is that? I tell you, my mama didn't raise me like that. I don't know who they think they are. Your Aunt Evelyn and I agree that there's something wrong with people like that."

I didn't know what kind of answer she expected from me. I wasn't in the mood to have a big long talk about neighbor relations with Mrs. Cross. So I just nodded one more time.

She started in again, lecturing me about manners and old-fashioned values. I stopped listening about two sentences in and was finally saved when her phone started ringing. "Oh, that'd by my sister Celeste. She's probably calling to complain about her bunions again. That woman just needs to get herself to a doctor instead of whining to me."

The phone rang again. "Yeah, well, then you should probably get that, Mrs. Cross."

She harrumphed—she was good at that. If there'd been a championship harrumphing contest, Mrs. Cross would have won, hands down. She got to her feet and plodded into the house, letting her screen door slap shut behind her.

I was all for being nice to my elders, but Mrs. Cross really pushed my patience to the end of its rope. Bunions? Manners? I'd rather talk about geometry.

Okay, maybe not.

I started to turn toward school again, but that eerie feeling returned now that I was alone again on the sidewalk. The St. Germain house sat silent and dark. It shouldn't creep me out—most of the houses on the block sat empty during the day because almost everybody had a job.

If I spent any more time here, I'd be late for school. And I still didn't know where Heather was.

None of that stopped me from moving steps closer to the weird old house. The wooden stairs were cracked and splintered, the paint on the porch railings peeling fast, as if it were trying to run away. Beneath the porch were slats in a crisscross pattern, but many of them were broken. Who would rent this place? I mean, it was one step away from condemnable. And if they were going to rent it, why not have it fixed up? Didn't they care?

Go to school, stop spying on the neighbors, I told myself. They were just strange, that was all. Everyone was entitled to a little strangeness. I had already half turned away when a dark brown lump caught my eye. I turned back, took another step, bent down, peered into the shadowy depths under the porch. Was that—

It was.

A shoe. A guy's shoe. Like a dress shoe. The kind a businessman wore. A businessman who might carry a briefcase? I tried to swallow a breath, but it got lodged in my throat.

The shoe was hardly dirty, as if it had just landed there recently. And it didn't look like something Adrien would wear. How had it ended up there? Why?

But more . . . whose was it?

I moved closer, my pulse thundering in my head, and reached out for the shoe. Above me, I heard a screech. A weird screech, nothing I'd ever heard before, and it sent a chill down my spine. I froze, looked up, but didn't see anything.

I reached again.

Something swooped down behind me and let out another screech. I jumped back. What the hell was that? I looked around and saw nothing. Didn't hear anything else, but something—some *thing*—had been there behind me. Some kind of bird? What was wrong with that thing?

The shoe glinted in the sun, as though it were taunting me to touch it. I reached out one more time, and just as I was about to grab it—inches away, so close I could almost smell the leather sole—a chattering sound erupted from under the porch . . .

And the shoe moved, then retracted, disappearing under the deck. As if the house had eaten it—or something under the house had. I shrieked, jumped back. My heart was a jackhammer, and I stared at the space where the shoe had been for a long, long time. Where had it gone? And what had dragged it under there? A dog, I told myself. It was just a dog.

Uh-huh. Didn't sound like a dog. That . . . chattering. Like a hundred birds on a telephone line. Except not with the happy kind of high-pitched gossip twitters. Something lower, meaner.

The sound had stopped. Nothing was moving. The house was as quiet as a tomb. If I'd had any doubts before that there was something weird about the St. Germain house, they were gone. Something was very, very, *very* weird there. No, not weird. *Wrong.* I just didn't know what.

Had the St. Germains done something to whoever had worn that shoe and carried that buried briefcase? Maybe . . .

Killed him?

Oh man, I was watching way too much *CSI*. This was suburbia, not the crime capital of the world. Neighbors didn't kidnap CEOs and kill them in their kitchens. Still . . . what was up with that shoe? And what had Adrien been doing the other night?

The curtain in the front window swished to the side. Oh, crap. I scooted away as fast as I could. Someone was watching me. The same person who had seen me before? It had to be Adrien's mother. I didn't hang around to find out—or to become the next thing dragged under that porch. I just turned toward school. Toward a place that was about a three on the Insanity Index.

Where that house was like a ten thousand.

I had to be seeing things. Had. To. Be. Hadn't Aunt Evelyn told me she was worried about my vision? I dug out my eye drops and squeezed a few into my eyes. Maybe my vision was deteriorating faster than the doctor had said it would. Yeah, but, like, decades faster?

Something told me that what I'd just seen had nothing to do with what was wrong with my eyes and everything to do with what was wrong with the St. Germains.

I heard the flutter of wings and I looked up. A bird circled the sky above me. Something big and dark. It was too far away for me to make out what it was, but I could tell one thing—

That sure as hell wasn't a pigeon.

It cried out, a long, almost screaming sound that made my skin crawl. Along the telephone lines, rows of black birds perched, their beady eyes watching me. Dozens and dozens of them.

I walked faster.

The bird kept on circling above me, letting out a cry every few seconds. I was nearly running now, and still, that bird was there. It was huge, with a wingspan of at least two feet and a long, skinny neck with a ring of feathers at the base. Oh my God. *A vulture.*

What was a vulture doing in my neighborhood? I didn't know much about them, but I did know they circled things that were dead.

Maybe there was a dead deer in the road nearby or something. That's what I told myself, even as the vulture tightened his circle. Around me. I crossed the street and looked up again. Even more crows sat on the wires, on the rooftops, like a silent army, just watching. A chill shuddered through me. Why were they doing that? What was going on?

I glanced back and forth between the birds and the road, trying to watch for my sister. Why had she gone in early? Since the accident, Heather, who used to love school, who had been so anxious to get here every morning, had changed. She used to be the one dragging me out of bed as if Mondays were

Christmas. She'd loved it all—the classes, her friends, drama, sports. Then, our lives turned inside out and she started getting to school later and later—if she went at all. Which was why I'd started making sure she went every day by going with her.

Then today, she just takes off on her own. The same day Adrien goes in early.

Coincidence? I didn't think so.

Above me, the vulture circled and circled, still calling out every few seconds. The sound creeped me out, and I hugged the right side of the sidewalk, trying to stay under the trees, trying to stay out of sight, but it didn't seem to do me any good. Everywhere I looked, everywhere I turned, there were those crows, staring at me. Majorly creepy.

For a minute, I thought the vulture was going to swoop down and land on top of me, but then, just as I reached the entrance to school, the bird veered off, back toward Adrien's house.

What the hell had that been about? For a second, I wondered if Adrien had sent the vulture and crows after me. But then, just as quickly, I pushed the thought away. For one, he couldn't control what wild birds did. And for another, why would he do something like that?

But . . . that vulture had come from the roof of his house, and those crows had followed along. I knew it had something to do with him. I just wasn't sure what.

CHAPTER 15

I hurried into school—finally away from those freaky birds—and almost collided with Sam. "Hey, Sam," I said. He had on a blue shirt today, which just made his blue eyes look even bluer. "Have you seen Heather?"

He shook his head. "I'm not her keeper."

I wondered what had him so snippy, but then he went on to say, "Everyone is talking about how she landed the role of Juliet in the school play. And guess who's playing Romeo?"

My heart sunk. Heather hadn't even told me about the play when we'd spoken last night. She was still shutting me out. "Adrien?" I guessed. He seemed like such a phony to me that I wasn't surprised he was a good actor. And he certainly had enough adoring fans.

"Are those two, like, dating or something?" Sam asked, a look of disgust on his face.

"I think so," I said, recalling that Heather had told me she was falling in love with Adrien. "She never tells me anything anymore." Why hadn't she told me about the play? Always, before, Heather would have come running in the door, shouting about how she'd gotten the female lead. She would have been reciting her lines over breakfast, making me play the other parts against her, searching through her closet for costume choices.

"What *is* it about him?" Sam asked.

"Maybe it's his cologne. Eau de hunk."

Sam laughed. "Maybe I should try some. Think they sell that at Hollister?"

"I don't think you need it."

Sam arched a brow and grinned. "Oh, really?"

My face heated. "Come on, you know girls like you."

"I'm not interested in girls . . . plural."

He didn't say anything more, and I wanted to ask what he meant, but I also wasn't so sure I wanted to hear the answer. "Well, either way, whatever Adrien is doing, it's working."

Sam looked down the hall at nothing in particular. "You know, Heather and I might be over, but I still care about what happens to her. If that loser hurts her, I'll . . ."

"You'll what?" I asked when he didn't finish.

"Kill him," Sam muttered under his breath.

Whoa. This was a whole new side of Sam, one I'd never

seen before. I started to ask him if he was serious when he turned toward me and flashed the smile I loved.

Sam started walking beside me, his height a natural crowd clearer. I tried to look over and around people for my sister. Nothing. I stopped walking for a second and faced Sam. "I've been, uh, thinking about you lately."

The words had just kind of blurted out. *Good going, Meredith.*

I really hadn't wanted to say that. I mean, last week, those words might have been okay, when I'd looked at Sam and seen just a friend. Just Heather's old boyfriend. But this week—

This week was different. I wondered what Sam would have said if my cell phone hadn't interrupted us yesterday.

"I mean, just because I was, like, worried about you," I said. Fast.

He grinned. "Worried? About me? Why?"

"You took the whole Heather thing pretty hard, and now that she's dating again, I, well . . ." I put out my hands. What was I supposed to say? I couldn't tell him the truth.

When I looked at Sam, I didn't see Heather's old boyfriend anymore. I saw a guy I liked. A guy I'd liked ever since he'd come over to hang out in our half-finished cellar and listen to CDs. A guy I'd been paying more attention to at the yearbook computer than I'd realized until just now.

The Bubble Bots weren't the only ones hoping for a smile

from cute boys. Or in my case, from one boy in particular. I looked at my shoes. A lot easier than looking at him. "I just didn't want you to start listening to Death Cab for Cutie songs and playing with razors, that's all."

Sam laughed and put a hand on my arm, and a zing ran through me. A powerful zing. One that spelled trouble. He was Heather's, not mine. I mean, hadn't he just mentioned how jealous he was, like, five seconds ago? And besides, she was my sister. There was no bigger betrayal than liking—or worse, going after—your sister's boyfriend. Old boyfriend or not.

"Don't worry about that, Meredith. How can I get depressed when I have people like you looking out for me?" He clapped a hand on my shoulder.

Like he would a buddy. Great.

"Yeah," I said, but the word came out shakily, and now I couldn't concentrate on anything but his eyes again. "I . . . uh . . . I should find my sister."

"And I gotta get to the office. Try to sweet-talk Mrs. Ronald into forgiving my tardies so I don't have to serve detention this week. I'm going to tell her I was helping my mom get my little brother ready for preschool. I was. Most of the time. The rest of the time, I was making a Mickey D's run. Those Egg McMuffins call to me, I swear."

"Those sandwiches are pretty powerful tempters."

"Not as bad as the fries." He smiled, and I wondered if he was talking about the fries we had shared. "Think I have a chance?"

"Oh, yeah, you should be good to go." Then I left, because when he'd smiled like that, a part of me had been hoping that smile had been just for me, not the dean of student services.

I put Sam out of my mind. One problem at a time. Find out where Heather was, then deal with the other mess I was creating. Not to mention the craziness happening in the house next door, if there was any.

It could, as the shrink would say, just be all in my head.

I started down the freshman corridor. Past the bundles of giggling airheads watching the upperclassman boys head for their lockers, past the teachers sneaking out the side door for one more smoke before the bell rang, past the trio of too-perky flute players trying to sell candy bars for Columbus Day or whatever holiday they were manipulating for new band uniforms.

No Heather. Where was she? She couldn't have run off, right? Skipped school again, like the last time? That day, I'd found her at the cemetery, curled up on top of our father's grave, crying her eyes out. A total mess. I would have called the shrink, and probably should have, except she'd promised me she wouldn't do it again. That she'd go to school and keep on moving forward, not get caught in this grief swamp again.

She'd seemed okay last night after we'd talked, but how did I know she didn't break down again and let the guilt over what had happened to Dad eat at her until the morning? That, and the weird cologne thing a couple nights before, could have been enough to push her over the edge. Man . . . I should have kept closer tabs on her this morning. My heart skipped in my chest, and I shoveled my way through the people blocking the hall. God, she wouldn't—

The crowd split, and I saw Heather's backpack, then her ponytail. Relief washed over me. I ran up, grabbed her shoulder. "Hey, where were you this morning?"

She turned around, slowly. All her friends were there, too, looking like a flock of leftover Woodstock hippies or something. Heather, though, she looked at me—and smiled.

Oh my God, Heather was smiling? Happy? I was so surprised, I almost forgot to breathe. It was such a total one-eighty from her usual school self, I could have sworn she'd been switched by aliens.

"Meredith," she said, smiling even more. "Sorry, we had an early rehearsal."

"Hey, no problem." I said, all casual-like, but worry began to gnaw in my gut. Something about Heather's smile looked too . . . freaky. Like, too happy.

I shrugged off the feeling. What was wrong with me? I couldn't be happy for her? Just a few days ago, I'd thought she needed a stay on the closest crazy couch. Now she was smiling, and I still worried? Maybe I was the one in need of a psychiatric intervention.

Or maybe I was just getting too weirded out because of the neighbors and what had happened with that freaky bird and the shoe a little while ago. Seriously, I was dancing on the edge here, and things were not making sense. Maybe that shrink had been right. Maybe my father's death was just now hitting me, making me see and imagine things that weren't real, and I needed a vacation or something. Or a whole lotta Prozac and a box of Ho Hos.

"I heard about you playing Juliet. Congrats," I said.

"Thanks, Meredith. It's definitely my favorite role ever, so far." That smile on her face widened so much that it nearly touched her ears, and she stepped back. When she did, I saw Adrien standing beside her, part of the crowd, but clearly more aligned with my sister than the rest of the planetary bodies orbiting her. Now I knew why Heather's friends had that goofy starry-eyed look going on. And why the Tweedle Twins were so pissed off. It seemed as if every single girl in school was standing there, just hanging on Adrien's every breath. His smile swept over the group like a wave, and the girls closed in even tighter. They were like cattle—*pathetic.*

I started to say something, when the bell rang and Mrs. Roland, the dean of crowd control, stepped out into the hall. "Everyone get to class. Don't start the day with a tardy." She shooed at the crowd until they started to scatter.

Before she left, I tugged Heather to the side, out of Adrien's earshot. "Listen, just watch out for that guy. I saw something weird at his house this morning."

"Weird like what?"

"There was this vulture and it followed me to school. It came from his roof. And there was this shoe that just got . . . sucked under the porch."

Heather rolled her eyes. "Meredith, seriously. You really think you saw a vulture today? And what'd you say, a disappearing shoe?"

"I know it sounds crazy, but—"

"Maybe you just need to go back to the eye doctor."

"This isn't because of that, Heather. I really saw these things."

"I don't want to be mean, but you and I both know one of the side effects of what you have is seeing things." Heather leaned in as she said it. "Maybe just throw in some eye drops or something."

"Heather?" Adrien said.

"I gotta go." That smile took over her face again, and then she and Adrien headed down the math hall, their heads close together, as if they were sharing a secret only the two of them knew. A couple of her friends tagged behind, but it was pretty clear they were hangers-on, not part of the conversation. Adrien had Heather in his own little world. I heard Heather laugh, the sound so unexpected that I stopped walking and listened for it again.

Then she rounded the corner and disappeared from sight. For an instant, I'd seen the old Heather. The one thing I'd been praying to see for months. Even though I had my worries about who Adrien St. Germain was, I found myself hoping Heather's new attitude would last. And wasn't like one of those oasis things in the middle of Despair Desert.

Cassidy came running up to me, practically dragging me down the hall. "Did you hear?"

"If it's about the play, I heard." Cassidy and I ducked into history class and took our seats. But that didn't stop Cassidy from gushing.

"Adrien is going to be Romeo." Cassidy hung over her desk, arms waving in excitement. "ROMEO! Do you know HOW COOL that's going to be?"

"Cassidy, it's just a play. I don't see the big deal."

She snorted. "It's a huge deal for your sister! *She* gets to be his kissing partner. LIFE IS SO NOT FAIR."

Heather kissing Adrien on stage? In front of the whole school? No wonder she had that dreamy look on her face.

"Every girl in school is going to be totally jealous," Cassidy said. "And wishing they'd tried out for Juliet. I heard that when Adrien got up there and played Romeo, there was MEGA chemistry with him and Heather. LIKE, SPARKS FLEW AND EVERYTHING."

That I believed. I'd seen it myself just a second ago. The problem—I didn't like the idea much. I shook off the feeling. It wasn't as though Heather were going to marry the guy tomorrow. Surely whatever thing she had for him would wear off soon.

"That's good . . . I guess." I pulled my history book out and plopped the massive paperweight onto my desk. At the same time, Adrien walked into the room, wearing, as always, his sunglasses. Apparently no one had said a word to him about that. Did he get away with it by claiming they were prescription or something? Or just by smiling that charming little grin?

Or was it to hide what I saw in his eyes?

But that hadn't been real. Totally couldn't be. I mean, I lived in a real world where I saw, touched, felt, and smelled reality. And in reality realm, people didn't go around with worms living in their eye sockets. Maybe Heather was right, and all this was because of my eyes.

When I'd been diagnosed with Fuchs' disease last year, the doctor had said it would be years before I was symptomatic. Fuchs', a.k.a. Fuchs' Corneal Dystrophy, was an inherited eye disease that, like, 1 percent of the population had. Made me a freak, if you asked me. Most people didn't find out they had it until they were older, but I'd gotten "lucky," the eye doc had said, when I'd had a couple symptoms after my dad died. Yeah, luck wasn't what I'd call it. Eventually, my corneas were going to swell and burst and I'd need a transplant from someone who'd died. Dead corneas—on every teenager's Christmas list.

Adrien slid into his seat, slouching a little in the hard plastic chair. Beside me, Cassidy sighed, as if a Greek god had just descended into Jefferson High School. Paula and Krystal dashed into the room, pausing for one sec as they passed Adrien's desk. "Hi, Adrien," they said at the same time, then giggled.

Cassidy launched into her whole "Adrien is Romeo" story all over again and got a bigger bang for her word buck out of Paula and Krystal. They were totally ready to stage a protest over the lack of available female leads opposite Romeo. As though they could rewrite the Bard's greatest work into a polygamy version, just to get a chance to kiss Adrien.

I pulled out my eye drops and squirted in a couple, just in case. And to focus on something other than the Adrien love fest around me.

"I'm thinking we should have a whole page in the year-book dedicated just to Adrien," Paula was saying. "A get-to-know-the-new-guy thing."

"Brilliance," Krystal said. "Meredith, you really should do that."

I glanced to my right. Adrien turned at the same time, as if he had read my mind, and smiled. A half smile, one that made Paula, Krystal, and Cassidy let out a collective "ooh" beside me. But for some reason, it only made the Pop-Tart I'd eaten that morning make an encore appearance in my throat. Because when he smiled, it was just like when that vulture had been watching me. Predatory. Waiting.

Hungry.

I looked away. The nausea settled. But the feeling that Adrien was watching me didn't go away.

He leaned over, almost onto my desk. "I've noticed," Adrien said, his voice so quiet, no one but me could hear him.

"Noticed what?"

"You've been . . . spying."

I swallowed hard. Oh God. He'd seen me? How? We'd seen him leave. I thought of the curtain flickering in the window and realized it must have been his mother who had seen us and then told Adrien. Still I stuck to denial. "No I haven't."

"Look all you want," he said. "But just remember the old saying . . ."

"What's that?"

"Curiosity killed the cat." He studied his fingernails. "It could kill you, too."

"What's that supposed to mean?" The question forced its way out of my throat.

Adrien just gave me that smile again and shrugged, then went back to his desk. I rubbed my arms, trying to get rid of a chill that refused to disappear. He knew I'd been watching him, and after what he'd just said, I had a feeling that put me in danger. What kind, I didn't know.

And I really didn't want to find out.

Mr. DeLue hurried into the classroom at the same time the final bell rang. "Good morning, good morning, good morning," he said, papers slipping from his grasp as he shuffled over and dumped his briefcase onto his messy desk.

Wendell called a good morning back. A few other people mumbled something that could have been a greeting but probably was something you'd write on a bathroom wall.

Mr. DeLue started writing on the board, listing important battles of World War I. Most of the class let out a mass sigh of boredom, while the few who cared about their grades got out their notebooks and started taking notes. I flipped open a three-subject Mead and began drawing a lame attempt at a flower. Anything to make me look busy without actually having to pay attention. And to keep my mind off what Adrien had just said. I didn't want to look at him, think about him, or let him know he'd bothered me at all.

My pen made loop after loop, circling into figure eights, crisscross, crisscross, the flower getting darker blue with each stroke. Beside me, Cassidy had her chin propped in her hand, her head turned toward Adrien instead of Mr. D., and this dreamy look on her face.

Mr. DeLue just kept droning on and on, his voice in major monotone. Boredom set over me, heavy and thick. Behind me, I heard someone start to snore. Heat multiplied in the room, the crazy AC doing everything it could to cook us for lunch.

Circle, circle.

"Battle of Mons."

Circle, circle.

"Vimy Ridge."

More circles.

"Verdun."

Just as I started another loop, I felt something skitter across my ankle. I jumped and looked down. Nothing there. Had to be the leg of my capris, blown up by the freaky AC.

"The German siege of Verdun," Mr. DeLue was saying, "was the longest battle of the First World War." He began to draw *x*'s and *o*'s—good guys and bad guys, I guessed—and then a bunch of lines back and forth between them, like chalk war games. "The original attack was postponed because of the terrible February weather, which allowed the French to hastily add reinforcements here"—he drew some more on the board—"but the odds were still terrible. One million Germans against two hundred thousand French."

"Mr. D.? Where was this, again? And how'd that affect the war?" One of the front-row suck-ups asked.

That launched Mr. DeLue into overdrive, the kind of teacher heaven that got his face flushed, his voice running in hyperspeed, and his chalk creating dust like a Snoopy Sno-Cone Machine. "Great questions, great questions. Here, let me show you."

Another tickling sensation on my ankle. I shook my leg and glanced down again, bending over my desk this time to see better. At first I didn't see anything, except a leg I should have shaved three days ago, but then—

A flash of black. And long, skinny dark insect legs.

I shrieked and jerked back in my seat, my heart exploding in my chest. The entire class turned to stare at me, yanked out of their war-induced stupor.

"Miss Willis? Is everything all right?" Mr. DeLue asked.

"Yeah. I . . . uh . . ." I could barely speak. It wasn't as though bugs scared me, it was more that I didn't expect to find one on my leg in the middle of history class. "I saw a bug. That's all."

Someone snickered behind me. Someone else said something about spraying me down with Raid.

Wendell perked up. He flashed me a helpful grin. "Bug? What bug? I'll kill it for you, Meredith."

Wendell Marks, ever ready to save the world.

"I'm fine, Wendell. It was . . . nothing." And when I looked down again, I didn't see anything. Whatever it was must have flown away.

That didn't stop Wendell from lurching out of his seat and collapsing on all fours beneath my chair. He patted the floor in a wild circle, as if my life were in mortal danger from whatever arthropod lurked below. "Give me your history book, Meredith. I'll smash that sucker for you."

"There's nothing there, Wendell. I told you, it's gone." Probably just a fly or a bee. Nothing.

Except . . .

It hadn't looked like either of those. The little bit of it I had seen had seemed . . . too big. The legs . . . too long. A shiver ran up my spine, but I ignored it. Tried to focus on the blackboard.

"Mr. Marks . . ." Mr. DeLue said, his voice a warning. "Let's stick to the battles of history, not of bugs. Please retake your seat."

Wendell nodded and slunk back to his chair. Just before he sat down, he picked up his copy of *World History* and flashed it my way, still ready to defend me from the insect world. Whoo. I could be the lucky girl taken care of by this Superman.

Mr. DeLue went back to the board. The class went back to being bored. I started drawing more circles.

The tickling started again. I kicked my leg, looked down—

And saw a massive black bug—holy crap, was that a bug or a small bird? The thing was humongous, with a black body and two sets of thick bright orange stripes on its back. A beetle? I thought it was, but whoa, it was huge. At least an inch long, a half inch thick—and sitting *on my freaking leg*. A scream traveled up from my gut, but fear squeezed my throat shut, and I sat there, totally paralyzed, my heart thundering in my chest, my breath caught. *Move—get off me!*

All six legs perched on my leg, their little feet . . . twitching. Then, I swore, the bug swiveled its egg-shaped head and stared at me.

I jerked back against my chair. Lifted my opposite foot and tried to brush the bug off. But then, just as I did, I noticed—

A dozen more just like it, arrayed beneath my feet. What the hell? Where had *they* come from? All of them looking at me, hidden under my desk, caught in a shadow, out of sight from everyone, I think, but me. I couldn't breathe, couldn't move. I looked around, sure someone else would see them, would scream.

But the entire class was going on as usual, looking about as excited as a convention of undertakers. The girls' eyes were fixed on Adrien, and he was looking at them, like some kind of staring contest. Not a one of the female pop was paying attention to Mr. DeLue. Or to me. Wonderful. I sat there, frozen, my gaze darting over to Wendell. My big hope—ha.

Notice the bugs, I thought, trying to send him a mental message. *Notice them.*

Wendell glanced my way. Sent me a thumbs-up.

Then turned back toward the board.

He hadn't seen them? Was he blind? Some savior he was. God. I glanced down again at the floor. The bugs hadn't moved. The one on my leg, the dozen at my feet. I shifted my legs, very, very slowly, moving them forward. *Shoo. Get out of here, you freaks.*

The bugs held their ground. I had to be imagining them. Had. To. Be.

I forced myself to stay in my chair instead of running out of the room, screaming like a total lunatic. I twitched right, left, watching the bugs, who were watching me.

No one saw them? Or were my eyes playing tricks on me?

I nudged Cassidy. "Hey."

"WHAT?" she whispered—or tried to.

"Do you . . ." Man, this was going to sound nuts if she said no. "Do you see that bug anywhere?"

Cassidy glanced down at the floor—looked right under my desk—then back up at me. She shook her head, but something seemed off to me. Her eyes had this . . . glassiness about them. As if she were drugged or something. Not her usual perky self. Before she even started talking, she had gone back to looking at Adrien. "No, uh, sorry, Meredith."

"Miss Cramer?" Mr. DeLue said. "Do you have something to add to our battle discussion?"

She hesitated a second, as if trying to figure out what Mr. DeLue had asked her, then Cassidy brightened. "No, Mr. D. I'm riveted. Really."

Mr. DeLue made a face and went back to the board. Cassidy went back to staring at Adrien. I looked under my desk again, sure that I'd see what Cassidy had seen—nothing.

But they were there. All thirteen of them. Staring at me.

Then the one on my leg started to move, its six feet scrambling fast, running like an itchy river down my leg. I could feel every step, every movement, and I reached down to swat it off, but it moved faster than I could, and I wanted to scream, but couldn't find my voice.

Oh my God, oh my God. Don't do that, don't, no, no.

I flinched, my hand finally making contact now—

And it bit my leg.

I clamped a hand over my mouth, keeping my scream inside. That had to have been real, didn't it? But if that was so, why couldn't anyone see the bugs? Why didn't Wendell— who glanced over at me again, a nerdy-to-the-nth-degree Clark Kent ready to take on the insect world for me—leap over here and smoosh these things?

Kill them. Get rid of them. Now, please. Get them off me. Please.

The rest of the world kept on turning—Mr. DeLue on to another battle, people scribbling in their notebooks, others sleeping on their desks, the air conditioner blowing hot air. The girls in the class watching Adrien's every breath as though he were a movie star.

Then, just as fast, the bug was gone. It leaped off my leg, joined the others. They perked up their heads, held position for one long second, and then, in one mass group, skittered off. I heard their feet clicking against the tile floor, like a hundred fingernails scratching against a chalkboard—eerie and high-pitched. One by one, they disappeared under the AC unit. When the last one was gone, I let out a breath. I lifted my right leg onto my left knee. Ran a hand up the side. And found a slight bump. A bite mark.

The thing really had bitten me. Oh my God. I hadn't imagined it at all.

The bell rang and I scrambled to my feet, collecting all my books in one messy pile. I couldn't get to the door fast enough—not even bothering to wait for Cassidy. No way was I going to stay in that classroom one second longer than I had to. At the door, Adrien caught up to me and put a hand on my shoulder. His touch was icy, like a frozen steak. "Everything all right, Meredith?"

"Yeah, I'm fine." My mind was swimming. How could something no one else had seen have bitten me? And why was the guy next door suddenly so concerned?

Adrien smiled, and his hand dropped away. "Good," he said. "Because you looked like the cat that got bitten by its own curiosity." Then he walked away.

And as he did, I swore I heard the same eerie chalkboard scratching sound walking right behind him.

CHAPTER 16

Heather hadn't been this happy in months. She dumped her book bag by the door, kicked off her shoes, then headed into the kitchen. "Hey, Mer."

Meredith looked up from her geometry book, but she seemed distant, not herself. Her hair was a mess, as though she'd run her fingers through it a hundred times. Her homework paper was blank, her pencil eraser chewed clear off. "Huh? Oh. Hey."

That was it? Nothing else? God, what was up with her sister lately? It was as if the two of them had switched roles, and now Meredith was the one walking around all sad and weird. "Did you have a good day? Because I sure did."

"Good day? No. I wouldn't call it that. At all." Meredith made a strange face and Heather thought she might say more, but she didn't. "Your new boyfriend said something really strange to me in history class."

Heather gripped the metal handle of the fridge, pissed that Mer could take her good mood and bring it from sixty to zero in, like, two seconds. Typical Meredith. Whenever Heather had something cool in her life, her older sister had to pick at it. Pick, pick, pick, and find something wrong. So she could come out as the smarter, better sister.

Like she had last night and this morning. Just when it seemed as though they were getting close again, Meredith had to rattle off all the reasons why she thought Adrien was wrong for Heather. God, didn't anyone in this family care that Adrien made her happy?

"He's just the new guy," Heather said. "That's what makes him different." *And makes you hate him,* she added to herself. *He's new and different and you hate him just for that.*

"I don't think so, Heather. I think you should be really careful around him. Today, he—"

Heather slammed the fridge shut, so hard the bottles in the door chattered against one another. "You're just jealous, Mer. Because he's giving me attention and not you."

"That's not it. At all. I'm just worried about you and who you're hanging out with. You don't understand what kind of person he is. I think he might be dangerous."

Heather marched forward, hands on her hips. "Oh yeah?" she said, almost in Meredith's face now. "Or are you just telling me all this because it's convenient for you? Leah told me about you going for burgers with Sam. How you two are hanging out together. All the time."

Meredith jerked back. "Heather, we're on yearbook together. And the burgers, that was nothing. Really. Just—"

"Just you trying to move in on Sam. I get it, really. Heather's all screwed up, so why not take advantage? Fine, have him. I don't care." She didn't even know why she was making such a big deal about it. She and Sam had dated, sure, but she'd felt as if he had been more of a friend than a boyfriend. She didn't care if he moved on. And if he was happy with Meredith, great. But for some reason, a surge of anger rose in her chest, sharp and hard. It was as though someone was whispering to her that she shouldn't let Meredith get away with this. That it was wrong and awful. And it was all Meredith's fault.

Except it wasn't, was it? Confusion warred in Heather. She thought of that empty place at the dining room table, an empty place that was all because of Heather's driving off the road. She wanted to scream, to cry, to punch something. God, she was such a mess.

"Heather, I would never—"

Heather suddenly felt angry in a way she never had before. Angry that things had changed, angry that she couldn't change them back, angry about everything. The hole in her chest, the one that had seemed as if it was starting to close, opened up again, and a rush of emotion poured in. "Just stay out of my life! Stop butting in all the time. You can't fix it. You can't fix me." She turned away and went to the window. When she did, she saw him.

Standing in his driveway, facing her. As if he'd been waiting all this time, just for her to come to the window. Joy burst in Heather's chest. *Adrien.*

"I already found the fix I need, anyway," she said, then skirted the sink, avoiding Aunt Evelyn as she came in with a clean load of laundry and asked what was wrong. Heather headed for the back door, for the path that led out of her yard and into the one next door. "And I'm not going to let you or anyone else get between us."

Adrien smiled.

How much simpler could this be? Here she came, of her own free will, crossing the lawn in slow, dreamy steps. She called his name, once, twice. She was his. And he'd barely had to do anything to wrap his spell around her. She wasn't like the other girls at school, where he had to concentrate to get them to pay attention to him while he whispered in their minds. But once his words captured their attention, he kept it, made them focus on him, not on what he was doing or whatever else might be happening around them.

And those treats he'd given Meredith today. Ah, how well his pets had behaved. He had been so proud of his birds and the beetles. Such smart, loyal creatures. Meredith had had a taste of what he could do. But she had so much more coming to her, if she kept on interfering.

Meredith was immune to his touch, his words. Why, he didn't know. He'd never met a young girl who could resist him. Their willing, open minds and blind vision saw only his youth, heard only his sweet words, didn't hear the message underneath and blocked the truth of what he was. But this one was different. And that difference worried him.

Either way, he would deal with her. And end the threat she represented.

Heather came toward him now, her face happy and serene. Adrien put out a hand, ready to draw her in, take her inside and introduce her to Marie, when the door opened again and the old woman—the aunt—stepped onto the back stairs. She cupped a hand over her eyes to block the sun and stared at him. Her eyes were cold, hard. Her opposite hand went to her hip, and he had the feeling they were almost in a standoff.

As if that hag could win against him. She had no idea what she was up against. What he could do. Every day, his powers grew stronger and found untapped wells of strength, spurred on by his desire for Heather.

Then Meredith came out and stood beside the ugly old woman. Ha. The sister now, too? When was she going to learn? She'd thought the birds and the bugs had been bad this morning? That was nothing. If she got in his way, if she interfered in his plan to have Heather . . .

He would bring all his wrath down upon her. Her and that worthless bag of skin that was her aunt. First, he would consume the aunt and make Meredith watch as he ate little pieces of her loved one right in front of her, a preview of her future. Then, once he had the Knowledge, he'd convert Meredith's sister into a zombie like him. Let her see her precious Heather become one of the flesh-eating walking dead.

Then he would throw Meredith to Marie. Watch her be torn to shreds. Adrien grinned. Ah, what a fitting end for those nosy, persistent neighbors.

The sister stared at him for one long minute before turning toward the girl. "Heather! Aunt Evelyn needs you to go to the store with her."

Adrien smiled at Heather. His power was certainly stronger. She kept walking. *That's right, my love, keep coming. This way, toward me. We'll be together. Just like you wanted.*

"Heather!" the old woman called. The two of them joining forces. Stupid people.

Adrien took three steps, closing the gap. "Heather, hello. Why don't you—"

"*Now,* Heather, or dinner's going to be late," the sister cut in, interrupting Adrien's sentence. Heather paused, turned toward the voice.

Adrien wanted to scream. He wanted to rush across the lawn and rip the sister's heart out. Eat it right there in front of her, while she watched with her last dying breath. His fists curled at his side, and he had to force himself to keep the friendly look on his face, to stay where he was.

Heather's steps faltered. The smile on her face dropped away.

"Heather, let's practice our lines," Adrien said, but the words underneath, the ones no one could hear but Heather, whispered the intoxicating mix—*come closer, come to me, you're so beautiful, so perfect, I want to make you mine.*

"I . . ." Heather hesitated.

"Heather!" The sister again. Adrien glared at Meredith.

Heather's gaze dropped to the ground—*no, no, don't look away, keep watching me*—and then it was over. Without looking at him again, she mouthed an *I'm sorry,* then turned and went back into the yellow house.

Adrien scowled. Bit back a roar of fury. The sister. That damned sister. He could take care of an old woman with his eyes closed, but this sister—

Her determination to eliminate him, to find out the truth about who he was—it was strong. So much stronger than anyone else's had ever been, in all the cities he had lived in, all the years he had walked the earth. He felt it, crawling along his skin. Behind him, he could feel Marie watching and almost hear her judgment. She would have told him to take the girl now, take the sister as collateral. But Marie—

She was sloppy. She'd made too many mistakes in her rush to regenerate. It was why they had left the last place and the one before that, both times with suspicions hot on their trail. Whispers surrounding them like a spider's web.

If they didn't do this one right, they'd lose it all. And Adrien did not intend to let anyone—not Marie, and certainly not Meredith—ruin his plans.

He would have his forever bride. No matter what.

CHAPTER 17

On Saturday morning, I slept in, late enough that my mother had already left to go shopping and took Heather with her. Normally Heather had no interest in being a part of Mom's spending sprees, but now that she had a new guy to impress, I guess she wanted some new clothes. Aunt Evelyn was sitting at the kitchen table, filling in a crossword puzzle. I grabbed a glass of juice and sat down with her. "Twitter," I said.

She glanced up. "What?"

I pointed at the crossword puzzle. "Ten across. The clue said, 'One hundred and forty characters.' That's Twitter."

"Like a bird?"

I laughed. "Yeah, something like that."

She penciled in the letters, then moved on to the next clue. "You'll have to make your own breakfast because I'm going next door in a minute."

"Next door? To the St. Germains' house? I thought you didn't like them."

"I don't. But Heather does. And because of that, I will try to get to know them." I started to protest but my aunt put up a hand. "Stop. I don't want to hear it. I know that boy has his problems. But maybe if we are the bigger people—"

"It's more than just problems, Aunt Evelyn. You know how you mentioned they had bug issues? Well, one of those bugs attacked me in class yesterday. There wasn't just one, either—there was, like, a dozen surrounding me."

"Dear," Aunt Evelyn began, a hand going to my shoulder, "are you sure you saw them? You know there was that one time you thought the wallpaper was coming off the walls . . ."

"That was before I got my eye drops, Aunt Evelyn. My eyes were dry and that made things fuzzy. But not this time. This was real. And I think . . . I think Adrien made the bug attack me." Okay, once I'd said it, the whole thing made me sound like the weird one. I wanted to take it back, but I'd already spoken the words.

She arched a brow. "How does anyone control bugs?"

"I don't know what he was doing, or how, but I know he had something to do with it." No way was I going to mention the birds, not after Aunt Evelyn had given me the are-you-nuts look and the must-be-your-eye-disease lecture.

"That high school is old and rundown, Meredith. I'm

not surprised it has an insect infestation. What I don't believe is that the neighbor had anything to do with it." She gave me a stern look, the one that said not to leap to conclusions without enough evidence to back them up.

"But, Aunt Evelyn, I swear—"

Aunt Evelyn put aside her crossword puzzle, then headed for the door, picking up a basket of muffins as she did. "Don't forget you have chores to do today."

"At least let me go with you."

"You, young lady, will stay here and clean your room." She held up a finger, cutting off my argument. "I want to be able to see the floor by the time I get back."

The door shut behind her. She waved through the window. Conversation over.

I got up and paced. Should I have let her go by herself?

She was just bringing muffins next door, for Pete's sake. The neighbors weren't going to do anything crazy over that. Aunt Evelyn was one tough cookie, too. If she saw a bug, she wouldn't freeze like I had—she'd squash it with one sensible, low-heeled pump.

"Yo," Tweedledee said as he came into the kitchen, all sweaty and smelly. Eww.

"Yo," Tweedledum repeated. Bunch of Einsteins, those two.

They drank OJ straight out of the carton. My stomach flipped. Gross, gross, gross.

"Where's our mother?" one of the twins asked.

"Went next door to take muffins to everyone's favorite neighbor. Speaking of which, I thought you guys were going to pummel him."

"We are," Tweedledee said.

"Yeah, we are," his brother echoed.

"Well, he's home." Give him an extra slap for me, I wanted to say. For the bugs.

"He is?" The twins looked at each other, then put down their OJ and laid the basketball on the counter. The three of us crossed to the kitchen window.

Adrien stood on the porch, talking to Aunt Evelyn. He had his door shut, keeping my aunt out in the heat. He was smiling, making all the right gestures, but there was just something wrong. Why not invite her in? The woman came bearing muffins, after all. What was he hiding?

"I want to pound him," one of the twins said.

"Yeah, but if we do it now, Mom will kill us."

"Yeah. We'll have to wait, I think."

"Yeah." Tweedledee pounded his fist into his other palm. "Get him when he least expects it."

Adrien looked across the yards. I could feel his gaze connect with mine, even through the constantly-on sunglasses. He smiled. Then he pivoted back to my aunt, took the basket, and waved her inside. She disappeared from my view, and for a second, I wanted to scream no, to drag her out of there. Something felt wrong, so wrong, but I couldn't tell what it was.

Beside me, the twins shrugged and looked at each other. "Best three games out of five?" Tweedledum said.

"Sure."

And just like that, they were gone, back to thump, thump, swoosh. Morons. Didn't they worry at all about their mother being in a house with a tank full of piranhas? With a guy who clearly had some kind of weird control over bugs? Maybe even a vulture?

I watched out the window the entire time she was gone. Ten minutes. Fifteen. Twenty. Finally, after thirty minutes, Aunt Evelyn came out of the house, sending a friendly wave back at Adrien. The basket of muffins was empty and she was smiling as she crossed back to our house.

"What a wonderful young man," she said as she came inside. "I'm so glad Heather is dating him."

What had happened? How could he have convinced her he was Mr. Perfect that quickly? "So now you like him?"

She shrugged. "He's sweet. I think we just misinterpreted his intentions." She wrapped her apron around her waist, then started getting things out of the cabinet. "You would do well to make friends with him yourself, Meredith. In fact, he's invited all of us over there for dinner tomorrow night."

CHAPTER 18

You're stupid," Marie hissed. "They'll find out what we are."

The offer had been made in haste, but now Adrien could see the wisdom of his plan. "Not if you're conveniently absent. Look at you. You're a mess. Getting worse every day."

And she was. Her skin had started to flake, falling off in large chunks that littered the floor, creating a Hansel and Gretel trail that made the beetles follow her in anticipation. She limped now, dragging one foot behind her, her movements exaggerated and slow. She'd become the clichéd zombie. A monster out of a movie. Something not fit for human sight.

"You can't do this without your 'mother,'" she said, the last word so filled with sarcasm, she spat it out.

He towered over her. "I can. And I will. And if you help me, I will bring a meal for you at the end of our neighborly dinner."

Her eyes widened. She licked her lips. "What . . . what kind of meal?"

"Something young. Something that still has fight in it. Something . . . delicious."

She shook with her craving for another meal, and he knew he could use that to his advantage. "When will I have a new body? I need . . . *need* a new body."

"Soon," Adrien soothed, the lie slipping easily from his tongue. "Soon, Marie, you will have everything you deserve. And then some."

CHAPTER 19

Heather tried on three different skirts, six pairs of jeans, and two pairs of capris before finally settling on a pair of skinny black jeans and a striped Hollister shirt that her mother had said made her look like Heidi Klum. She wasn't so sure about that, but it looked the best out of everything she had and she definitely wanted to look her best tonight.

She spritzed on some perfume, slid some lip-gloss onto her lips, then brushed her hair for the four hundredth time. Ready.

Or, as ready as she could be, considering her stomach was doing cartwheels. She glanced out the window, but from her room, she could see only the corner of Adrien's house. She wished she had Meredith's room. Then she'd have a direct view.

She hurried downstairs and waited by the front door for the rest of her family. God, she hoped they didn't make her late. The twins came first, both of them looking as if they were heading for an execution. Aunt Evelyn followed behind them.

"You boys be nice," she said.

"Why? We don't even like him," Ted said.

"Because we are nice people," Aunt Evelyn said. "And Adrien isn't as bad as you've made him out to be. You just need to give him a chance."

Aunt Evelyn shot Heather a smile, then put a hand on her arm. One of those I'm-on-your-side touches. Heather didn't know what had happened with the muffins yesterday, but whatever it was, she was glad. *Finally* someone in this family was glad she was dating Adrien.

Her mother came around the corner, wearing a new outfit. Everything, from her shirt to her shoes, had been bought yesterday. Mom paused by the mirror, checking her appearance.

Finally, Meredith came downstairs. "I still don't see why we have to do this," she said.

Aunt Evelyn made the don't-argue face and opened the front door. Like a bunch of ducklings following a mother duck, they marched along behind her, down the sidewalk and up to Adrien's front door. Heather stood beside her aunt, shifting her weight from foot to foot, way nervous now about meeting Adrien's mother. Would she like her?

The door opened, and Adrien stood there, looking like he always did. Meaning, totally hot. He had on his jacket, white T-shirt, jeans, and, of course, his sunglasses. She knew the guys at school thought it was weird that he always wore sunglasses, but Heather loved it. She thought it gave Adrien an air of mystery.

"Welcome to my house," he said, then waved them in. As they passed by him, he reached out for Heather's hand and gave it a little squeeze.

A charge ran through her and she swore she could hear him whisper, *I missed you. I'm so glad you're here. Please don't leave me again.*

"My mother, unfortunately, couldn't be here tonight," Adrien said. "She had a . . . family emergency."

"Oh, that's such a shame," Mom said. "I know we were all looking forward to meeting her."

Adrien smiled. "I'm sure. But we will still have a pleasant dinner without her."

As she entered the house, Heather looked around. The space was meticulously clean, almost bare of furniture. Against one wall two fish tanks glowed light blue in the room. "These are cool," Heather said, pausing by the tanks. "What kind of fish are they?"

Before Adrien could answer, Meredith cut in. "They're piranhas, aren't they?"

"Why, yes, Meredith, they are," Adrien said.

"Really?" Heather drew her hand back, even though the fish couldn't bite through the glass.

"Those are dangerous, aren't they?" Mom said.

"Cool!" The twins pressed their faces to the tank. "Will they, like, eat us and everything?"

Adrien chuckled. "Oh, I doubt that. I fed them well enough so that they won't be interested in you." Adrien crossed to the tank and dipped a finger into the water, trailing it slowly back and forth. The fish followed the digit but didn't bite. "They're beautiful creatures, don't you agree?"

"Only if you like cannibalistic animals," Meredith said.

"Meredith!" Aunt Evelyn said. "Be polite."

Heather watched Adrien's finger going back and forth, back and forth. The fish, just watching, trailed its path. Why didn't they bite him? At least come up and nibble at his finger? Even the goldfish she used to have had done that. "What are you? Doctor Dolittle?"

Adrien lifted his finger out of the water, shook off the droplets. "Doctor who?"

"You know, the guy who could talk to animals?"

"I've never heard of him. Where does this man live?"

She laughed again. "In some book. And an Eddie Murphy

movie. He's not real, Adrien. It was a joke . . . and now that I had to explain it so much, not a good one. Sorry."

"No, you were fine. It was me."

The twins were mesmerized by the fish and started tapping the glass. Adrien scowled. "I wouldn't do that if I were you," he said. "I'd hate to see you make them . . . upset."

"Why? Cuz they might bite you?" Ted said.

"Oh, they wouldn't bite me. The fish and I have an understanding. And although they are well fed, I can't control what they would do to you if you angered them."

The twins backed up. A lot. Adrien clapped a hand on each of the twins' shoulders. "Why don't we eat now?" He gestured toward a room on the right, where a table and chairs were waiting. "Please, have a seat."

As they walked into the dining room, Heather took one last look at the two fish tanks, her gaze lingering on the piranhas. That was just too weird. She'd heard of people who had a Venus flytrap on the kitchen windowsill—one of those three-dollar plants you picked up in a novelty shop and fed a bite of hamburger to every once in a while, just for chuckles—but had never, ever known anyone who kept cannibalistic fish in his living room.

And what's more, played with danger by sticking his hand right into the tank.

Then there was the Doctor Dolittle thing. Everyone had heard of him, right? The movie had been some megablockbuster, but more than that, the story was famous everywhere. Heather remembered hearing her kindergarten teacher read it to her and loving it so much—back in the days when she'd wanted to grow up and be a veterinarian—that she'd begged her father to buy the book. Made him read it to her at bedtime every night for a year straight.

Thinking of her father sent a stab of pain through her, a rush of tears to her eyes. She stumbled. Adrien caught her. "Are you all right, Heather?"

"Yeah, yeah."

No. I'm not. But if I tell you . . . you'll leave me, like everyone else has.

"I won't," he whispered. "Ever."

Had he read her thoughts? Or had she said that out loud?

"So, what's in the other tank? More flesh-eating fish?" Meredith said.

Heather wanted to hit her. God, she hated her family. Everyone but her aunt was being totally rude. But Adrien just gave Meredith a patient look as everyone slipped into chairs and he took the one at the head of the table. "You are quite inquisitive, Meredith. Have you ever considered working in espionage?"

Heather muffled a giggle behind her hand.

"Meredith," Aunt Evelyn scolded again. "Be nice."

"Yes," Mom chimed in. "We're here for a nice, neighborly dinner. You children behave." As though they were five or something.

"So, Adrien, what's for dinner?" Heather asked, changing the subject from the fish.

"I'm not much of a cook," he said with a smile, "so I took the liberty of ordering out. The delivery man brought something I'm sure is very delicious." He rose and crossed into the kitchen, then returned with several containers of pasta dishes and one big salad. He passed the first bowl of noodles to Heather, who was sitting on his right, and again, she felt his arm brush hers.

Heard that whisper between them.

You look beautiful. Even more beautiful than Juliet.

She barely ate a bite. Everyone around her talked, but she hardly heard them. Adrien would talk to her and sometimes touch her, and when he did, she felt that same amazing tingle and heard his voice in her head, and she just . . .

Stopped thinking about anything but him. All she heard was his voice in her head. All she saw was his face. She couldn't think, couldn't eat, couldn't even form a sentence that didn't center around him. Was this what love was like? If it was, she was so, so, *so* in love.

Too soon, everyone finished eating. She noticed Adrien hadn't touched a bite, and that made her smile. Well, she guessed she wasn't the only one affected by their contact.

A thump sounded from somewhere in the house. Then another. "Yo, what's that?" Ted said. "You got a raccoon or something?"

Something flashed across Adrien's face, then was gone before Heather could tell what the emotion had been. "Perhaps. I need to go see what that is. Will you excuse me?"

In the next instant, he was gone, and Heather was left with her family. She shouldn't have felt lonely, but she did. All she could do was wait for Adrien to return.

CHAPTER 20

The blow knocked three of Marie's teeth out of her head. She reeled backward, her arms pinwheeling. For a second, Adrien thought she would lose her balance and topple to the floor. He prayed she would. Prayed she'd fall—and shatter into a million pieces, and then he'd finally be rid of her. But at the last second, Marie recovered her balance and righted herself.

"What were you thinking?" he said, his voice low, his fist raised for a second attack.

She cowered. Then straightened. Still trying to be the leader. He had to give her credit for that. Marie didn't go down easily. She was still fighting to stay on top, even though she knew the cause had already been lost.

"I needed this thing." Marie swiped a hand toward the man hanging from the chains, her clawlike fingers stripping a slice of his flesh as she did. He screamed, but the sound was poured into the thick gag stuffed into his mouth. The rattling increased. Followed by sobbing and several pained moans. The scent of decay filled the air. The man was old, paper-thin, his skin flaccid with age—too old, really, to be much good for anything. They'd have to eat him soon, before he spoiled. Adrien's nose wrinkled in distaste. He preferred his prey fresh, young, their blood pumping with a strong life force. Perhaps he'd give his portion of the man to the piranhas and the hyenas. They were far less choosy about what filled their digestive track than he.

"You can't just *take* one. Especially so soon after I've hunted and brought us two in a single week. In a place like this, it will be noticed. You know that."

"No one will miss this one," Marie said. "No one at all. He couldn't even walk. He was so easy to take. All I had to do was drag him." She ran a hand down the man's bare chest, taking another slice of flesh with her, then licked the remnants of blood and skin from her fingers.

The man screamed again, bucked against the chains binding him in place, but it was no use. His ankles were looped together, his wrists connected to the thick, heavy chain hanging from the ceiling. After a couple jerks, he gave up, his strength already depleted. The blood had drained from his upper body, and Adrien could tell he wouldn't last long. A few hours, a night. If that.

This one wouldn't be any fun. It would be pitiful.

"Do you realize what would have happened if that girl had seen him? They've already heard him. If one of them comes down here . . ."

Marie took a step forward, her eyes bright with a fury that she held in check. "I wouldn't have to eat him if you just gave her to me. Stop delaying the inevitable."

"I'm not. I'm waiting for the right time."

Marie watched him for a long moment, then let out a derisive snort. "You let her get to you, didn't you? You've started to *care* about her."

The way she said the word made it sound like a curse. Like a disease that he needed to have excised from his body. But she was right—caring for a human was a dangerous thing. The biggest mistake he could make. He needed to rid himself of that emotion so that when it came time for Heather to make the transformation, Adrien wouldn't think of what it would cost her.

How painful it would be for her to leave her family behind.

How painful it had been for him to leave his behind. Yes, he'd been dead when he'd been raised, but once he'd touched the ground again, oh, how he'd wanted to go home, to see his mother and father one more time. Marie had convinced him it would be better for everyone if he never returned. What parents wanted to see their son as one of the walking dead?

"I don't care about her," Adrien lied.

But he did. How could he want her for his forever companion if he didn't? He could do this, he told himself, could turn her into a creature like him. He could keep his emotions in check when he needed to.

Marie snorted. "Then why do you work so hard to curry the favor of the humans? Having them over for dinner, indeed. Humans are the *meals,* Adrien. Remember that. And stop trying to play nice with them. It's a waste of our time. You know what we are and what we do." She leaned in toward him. "We come, we devour, and then we move on. It's the way of our type."

"Maybe it's time for a different way."

"That's foolishness. I went along with this plan of yours"—she gestured toward the rooms above them—"because you begged me to act like them. But it's nothing but a waste of our time."

Adrien's hand curled into a fist. So tight, his fingernails dug into his palms and would have drawn blood if he'd had any. Quickly, he released his fist. It wouldn't do him any good to harm this body. He liked it and knew the girl did, too. He needed to make it last.

"It's far from a waste," he said. "Don't you want more than this empty life we live?"

She looked at him, her eyes blank, confused. "What more? There is nothing more, Adrien. We have our freedom. We have eternity. Isn't that enough?"

He thought of the girl. Of her long brown hair, her wide, open smile, and her deep, dark eyes, filled with a soul that called to him. Even down here, he could feel her loneliness, like tentacles, reaching for him. "No, Marie. It's not enough."

She cupped his jaw, her half-bone, half-skin hand scratching against his chin. Beside them, the old man twitched and whimpered, but they ignored him. "You foolish boy. You think you have choices? There are none. We were created for one purpose. To be slaves that toil night and day, never needing water or food or a bed to sleep in. How quickly you forget that I was the one who took you from that existence."

He scowled. "I haven't forgotten."

"It seems to me you have." She pointed upward. "Because now, when we have such delicious treats within our grasp, you stand here talking of grand ideas like fitting in. Take them, Adrien, take them *now*." She began to drool, large drops of spittle puddling onto the floor at her feet. "Bring those girls to me."

"No. Two at once is too much," he said to Marie slowly, as if talking to a child. She was always acting so rashly, making such stupid decisions. She was the whole reason they'd had to run from Boise. And then there'd been Panama twenty-two years earlier. Marie's greediness had brought them more trouble than Adrien could count.

In Boise, only he and Marie had escaped, and only because they had chosen to sacrifice the other two. The bullets of the frenzied mob had punctured the others' brains, immobilizing them until they could be tossed into the fire. He could still hear their screams as they died in that final, irreversible death. Didn't Marie realize that could be them if she wasn't careful?

He would have to do something about Meredith, but when the time was right. At dinner, Meredith had been quiet. Too quiet, if you asked him. That kind of silence never boded well.

"You need to listen to me, Adrien," Marie said. "She's *mine.* I will open her mouth and pour my soul into her body." She ran a hand down her waist, sliding her palms over skin that was so rotted, it nearly peeled off beneath her touch. Adrien had to force himself not to look away. "Then I will have that sweet new skin for my own. I'll be beautiful again."

"You—" Adrien yanked up Marie's hand, closing his fingers so tightly around her wrist that he could feel them sinking into the soft, rotting flesh. He wanted to kill her now so badly. She was so stupid, so idiotic. "You've been foolish,

Marie. Wasteful of the bodies you have had. It has made you weak and dangerous to our way of life. I will not allow you to ruin everything we—no, I—have worked so hard to create. And everything I am working for now."

"Let go!" She tried to wrest away from him, but it was a waste of effort.

Adrien pushed at the wriggling man. He smelled of despair, of his own waste. A horrible specimen. Completely disgusting. Clearly a homeless man, the weakest prey of all, the lowest dregs of meals. That alone showed Marie's declining abilities. In the old days, she'd have taken down a thirty-year-old man in the prime of his life. "We can't let him go now," Adrien said. "He'll just lead the police to us. We might as well eat him."

The man shrieked again, flailed, a butterfly caught in a web. His tears mingled with the filthy sweat coating his skin. It would have been laughable, if Adrien were in a laughing mood.

Marie licked her lips. She opened her mouth, already waiting for that first bite. "I want to eat him now. Let him scream as I devour his brain."

Adrien twisted her wrist, bending it back, stopping before it broke. Using enough pressure to let Marie know he could, with no effort, leave her disadvantaged. Never able to hunt again. For the first time, Adrien saw something in Marie he'd never seen before—

Fear. Of him.

"How dare you?" She tried to break free, but he held tightly.

"I'm the one in control now, Marie. You know it. I know it. You do what I tell you to. Nothing else." He bent her wrist even farther, until it was on the verge of snapping. She nodded, just once. "I make all the decisions now. Whether you get to have this revolting morsel of nothing . . . or whether I simply throw him, piece by piece, to the hyenas, the fish."

"You . . . you wouldn't." Drool slipped out of her mouth, dripped onto the concrete floor.

Adrien saw her eagerness, her hunger, and realized how he could get the Knowledge. A smile curved up his face. He cupped Marie's jaw. "You may keep your prize, my dear Marie—"

"Thank you," she said, her contriteness coming with a bite. Reluctant still.

Oh, she would learn.

"But there is a price to pay for what you have done. For how you have ruined my plans."

"A price?"

He lifted the man's hand to Marie's nose, allowing her to take in the scent of a meal. She opened her mouth, flicked out her tongue, tasted his wrinkled skin. "You give me the Knowledge that I seek," Adrien said, "or I will eat this meal in front of you and never hunt for you again. I will let you starve. Slowly, painfully." He yanked the hand away from her. "Nor will I bring you another body when it is time for you to shed this one you have so badly abused."

Though it filled him with distaste to eat something so rotted with age and filth, he bit down on the man's hand, devouring two of his fingers in a single bite. The man's body contorted with pain, but the gag suffocated most of his scream. He kicked his bound legs, a mermaid trying to swim away. A flare of pity ran through Adrien. It would actually be a kindness to devour him. Adrien stepped back, swiped at his mouth, and dared Marie to counter him.

Hunger contorted Marie's features. Still, she shook her head. "I won't—"

He slid between her and the prey, blocking her view. "You will. Or you will go back to being one of the dead. You will rot in the ground for all eternity while I walk among the living."

Anger flashed in her eyes, hardened the lines in her face, but she took a step back and lowered her head. Deferring to him. Finally. "I'm so hungry, Adrien."

He turned back to the man. As he did, he realized the man had died. Probably had a heart attack. Scared to death, literally. Too bad. Meals were always better eaten before their hearts stopped beating.

He reached up, released the dead man from the chains that had bound him, and held the body out to Marie. "Then by all means, eat, Marie. But be sure to take your prize to the other side of the room to enjoy. We wouldn't want anyone to see you . . . dining."

Marie smiled.

"Tonight, you may have your fill. Tomorrow, you will tell me everything."

She took the man, then paused before she began to eat and nodded once. Only once.

But it was enough.

Soon, Adrien St. Germain would have everything he'd ever wanted. An eternal life and the girl he loved by his side to share it. Just before he went back upstairs, he ripped a chunk off the man and stuffed it into his mouth. As he did, he imagined the pathetic creature was—

Meredith Willis.

That brought him a satisfaction no meal ever had.

CHAPTER 21

As soon as Adrien left the table to go "investigate" that raccoon or whatever he was calling that noise, I pretended I had to go to the bathroom and ducked out of the dining room. My family barely noticed I was gone. The twins were grumbling about Adrien putting on a macho show for all of us with the fish, my aunt was defending Adrien with Heather chiming in, and my mother was wondering out loud if we needed to buy a fish tank to jazz up the foyer.

I cut through the kitchen. Just before I ducked out the back door, I paused. Something didn't look right in this room, but I couldn't figure out what. I mean, it was clean—ridiculously so. Not one dish, not so much as a saltshaker, sat on the countertops. I took a couple steps to the right and pried open one of the cabinets.

Empty. Completely bare. No cereal, no soup, no plates. Nothing at all.

I opened another one. Same deal. What the heck?

Okay, so he'd said he wasn't much of a cook, but everyone had Cocoa Krispies or something. Some junk food at least. I wanted to look more but had no idea how long Adrien was going to be gone. I wanted to know what that thump was. I was not buying the raccoon theory.

A few seconds later, I was outside. I moved around the side of the house and nearly ran into a squat red container tucked between the shrubs. *Danger* was written all over it, right above the label "Acid."

Acid? What on earth? I couldn't think of a good reason for having that around. Didn't matter. I had more important things to deal with, like what that sound had been. I had only a few minutes at most before Adrien returned to the table. I ducked around the house to the basement window without a curtain, the one I had looked through days earlier. Whoever had taken down the curtain had forgotten to put it back. I flattened to the ground, then peered inside. At first I saw nothing. Then, a flash of something—or someone—in the cellar. Adrien?

No. Whatever I'd seen had been too pale. Too thin.

The hairs on the back of my neck stood up. I strained forward to get a closer look.

Oh my God. Oh, no.

I stuffed a fist into my mouth, bit down on my hand. At first I didn't believe what I saw. It was too . . . horrible. Too unreal. But then, as the bright light of the setting sun shifted and more of the cellar's horror came into my view, I knew I was seeing exactly what I thought.

A man—elderly, frail, helpless—bound and hanging by a chain from the ceiling. Metal cuffs held his wrists, dangled him above the floor like a deer waiting to be gutted. Blood dripped from gaping wounds running down his side. They looked fresh. Painful. Horrible. Adrien stood beside him and talked calmly to some woman. His mother, I presumed. Except she looked like crap. Her skin hung slack off her body, her hair was so thin I could see her scalp, and she was missing most of her teeth.

She looked horrible, so grotesque that I had to swallow hard to keep from hurling. It was awful, terrifying, unreal. I wanted to run away, to block the image of her decaying body, but I stayed glued to where I was. God, what was wrong with her? Cancer?

The two of them were just standing there, conversing as though there was nothing going on at all. Nothing unusual about a man being freaking *tortured* in the basement. Then I saw the worst thing of all—Adrien took down the man's body and handed it to his mother, and she bent over, then took a bite out of it.

Not just a nibble, but the kind of bite that said she was ravenous for his skin. A hunk tore off and filled her mouth. Immediately after, Adrien reached out and tore a chunk of skin off the man and stuffed it into his mouth.

Oh. My. God. They were eating him?

A scream raced up my throat. I clamped my hand over my mouth at the last second, holding the sound in before it escaped and alerted Adrien and his mother to my presence. I fumbled for my cell phone in my back pocket, got it out, and pressed 9-1. I was about to press 1 again when I realized—

My sister—my whole family, in fact—was still inside that house. With Adrien.

If I called the cops and they put on the red alert, complete with sirens and lights, Adrien and his mother would freak. What if they went after Heather and my family next? Took one of them hostage or something? Or ate that old man before the cops got inside? It would be all my fault, there'd be no evidence, and I'd have made a really bad situation worse.

I'd already seen bad enough. I couldn't imagine worse. And here my sister was, sitting at his dining room table picking at takeout dinner, smack in the middle of bad.

I couldn't risk it. I'd call later, when my family was safe at home.

I shoved the cell back into my pocket and dashed back inside. From the hall, I could peek into the dining room. Heather's seat at the table was empty, the glass of water abandoned. My heart stopped. Oh God, oh no, they already had her. They were going to take her down into that cellar and—

"Adrien?"

I heard Heather's voice from somewhere in the house. First floor, I thought.

"Adrien? Where are you?" Her voice again—closer to the front of the house.

I started sweating. A couple windows were open—a concession, I think, to having guests, because the St. Germains had never opened a window before—but it wasn't making much of a dent in the temperature. Didn't these people feel the heat? It was, like, ninety degrees out right now.

I went down a hall and found Heather near a closed door. "Heather," I whispered.

She turned, her mouth dropping open when she saw me. "Meredith, where did you go?"

"Come on, we have to get out of here. Now."

"What? Why?"

"Adrien and his mother, they have a prisoner in their basement. Some old guy. Hanging from the ceiling by a chain." I grabbed Heather's wrists, as if I could haul her out of the house myself. "I don't even know how to tell you what they're doing with him, but it's sure as hell not having a tea party."

"You're lying to me." She yanked her wrists out of my grip and started to turn away.

"No, I'm not. I swear. Please, come with me. I'll show you."

She hesitated.

I glanced at the cellar door. Listened hard. I didn't hear anything from Adrien or his mother, but that didn't mean they weren't standing right behind that door listening to us—or on their way up the stairs. "Heather, please. You have to come out with me now. If I show you what I saw, will you believe me then?"

"If this is just some trick to—"

"It's not, Heather, I swear. Please, just take one look in the window with me. It'll only take a second. And then you can go back to dinner if you want." Fat chance I was going to let that happen, but I didn't elaborate.

Her eyes met mine, and for that moment, we were sisters again, just like we used to be. "Okay," she said.

I hauled her out of that house as fast as I could and then over to the window where I'd been just a few minutes before. The whole time, though, I worried. What if Adrien and his mother saw us? They could still come after me—or Heather.

But if I didn't show her, she'd never believe me. And maybe seeing what Adrien was capable of would finally make her face reality and stop thinking this guy was all that.

"We have to be quiet. I don't want them to know we're out here." I took her hand and pulled her down to the ground, and then I pointed. "Here. Look."

Heather bent down and peered into the window. I waited, a heartbeat, two, for Heather to cry out, to scream, for her to jump back in horror.

"What am I supposed to be seeing, Meredith?"

"What do you mean, what are you supposed to be seeing? There's an old guy in there. I think they're torturing him."

"Uh . . . Mer? I see a bunch of boxes. Some weird-shaped crates. No old guy." Heather got to her feet and brushed the dirt off her knees. "Are you sure you saw him?"

I dropped to the ground and looked into the cellar.

Nothing. No Adrien or his mom. No guy being tortured and eaten. The cellar was empty, dusty, and making a total liar out of me.

"He was there, Heather. I swear. I saw him."

"Whatever. God, get your eyes checked, will you?" My sister let out a gust, then turned away. "I don't know why you hate Adrien so much." She pivoted back toward me, and her face changed, pinching into one that said the moment of sisterly love was way over. "Or why you keep trying to ruin my life. Just when I finally find something good—someone good—you want to take it away." She shook her head. "I hate you. Just stay away from me."

Then she stomped off. Right back into the house. I followed after her, calling her name, but stopped when I saw Adrien watching us from the window. He gave Heather a smile.

Then dropped me an icy glare that said he knew what I had been up to. And that payback was going to be a bitch.

CHAPTER 22

I called the cops as soon as I got home Sunday night. Put in an anonymous tip that I thought the people at that house were holding a hostage. A squad car came out, and a female cop got out to talk to Adrien. In five minutes, she was smiling at him and waving goodbye. Never even went into the house to investigate.

Had I imagined it? Or had that woman cop fallen under the same Adrien spell as every other girl in town?

The next afternoon, Sam stood in my kitchen, doing what only Sam could do—be a good friend. I had been a little freaked out when I'd gotten home from school to an empty house, with who knows what lurking next door. My mother was either working or shopping—she didn't tell us anymore. My sister, probably at play practice. The twins were at a b-ball scrimmage, and Aunt Evelyn had gone to the grocery store. So I'd called Sam, asking him to come over because I really needed some company. Almost as soon as I hung up the phone, Sam had been at my house, tall and solid and dependable.

He walked in, took one look at me, and asked if I was okay. I started to cry.

I never cry. Ever. Even when my dad died, I'd bucked up, kept the tears in check. Heather had been such a mess, and my mother had been a walking zombie, so I just kind of held in there because it felt as though someone had to keep it together. But when Sam did the care-and-concern thing, my emotional Jenga blocks came tumbling down, and before I knew it, I was a slobbering mess and Sam had me in a hug.

It felt good. Really good. He was warm and strong. He didn't let go. Didn't back up. Just held me until my tears soaked his shirt. I stepped away. "Thanks. Uh, sorry about your shirt."

He shrugged. "I have more."

Oh, man. Three words and I knew I was hooked. Why Sam? Why couldn't I have fallen for someone else?

I put more distance between us, heading to the fridge for a Coke I didn't want or need. "You, um . . . want some pizza rolls?" I said, just so he'd stay. I didn't care if it was right or not to lean on Sam's shoulder. I just needed someone . . . normal to talk to. Someone who would talk back to me. Not like my mother, who'd just throw another Nordstrom bag at me, or Heather, who'd perfected ignoring me. Or my friends, who wanted only to talk about how hot Adrien was.

"Cheese stuffed in dough?" Sam grinned. "It doesn't get better than that."

"Or worse for you."

"Hey, we're teenagers. We're supposed to eat like crap."

I crossed to the fridge, took the pizza rolls out of the freezer, then dumped them onto a plate and popped them into the microwave.

"Mer, you look good no matter how many pizza rolls you eat," Sam said.

A warm feeling came over me and I had to turn away so he wouldn't see me blush. "Thanks." I got the pizza rolls out of the microwave and placed the plate in front of Sam. "Need anything else?"

"A little company." He pointed toward the other chair. "It's no fun getting fat alone."

I laughed and sat down. As much as I wanted to keep on with the light pizza roll kind of talk, I knew I had to get to the point. "There's some stuff I need to tell you. About Adrien."

Sam popped a pizza roll into his mouth. "Like what?"

I told him about the bug biting me in class, about seeing Adrien bury that briefcase, about the shoe, and then, finally, about the old man who had been there—and then had been gone. "I think they were eating him, but no one does that, do they?"

He shook his head. "Eating or not, what you just told me is not normal, Mer."

"I agree."

Sam ran a hand through his hair and sat back. "What do you think is going on?"

"Either I'm totally paranoid or there's something up next door. But every time I try to figure out what it is, someone—or something—tries to scare me off."

But was that really what was happening? Could this all be some weird symptom of my Fuchs' disease? Could it just be my imagination working overtime? Hadn't that shrink said I'd have some kind of posttraumatic stress? That at any time losing my father could catch up with me and pound my mental health into the ground?

That's what I got for trying to be the strong one. For not crying. I should have had a meltdown six months ago, and then maybe all this wouldn't be happening. Maybe.

It all just seemed so confusing. Swirling in my head with a lot of other junk. Right now, I didn't know which way was right or left, or if I was just—

Crazy.

I got up to get a drink, then turned back to the table. As I did, I caught a glimpse of the newspaper out of the corner of my eye. "Oh my God."

"What?"

I slapped the paper down in front of Sam and pointed to the headline on the front page: "Family Worries About Local Businessman, Missing for a Week."

There was a small photo in the corner of the story of a smiling guy, midthirties, in a suit. Not the guy I'd seen hanging in the basement. But definitely a guy who could wear a shoe like the one I'd seen. Carry a briefcase.

"Meredith, this could just be a coincidence." But even Sam didn't sound convinced.

"I should have called the cops back. They didn't even check the house or look in the basement or anything. I mean, what if Adrien and his mother had had something to do with this guy's disappearance and the old guy I'd seen was their second victim?"

"Maybe." He fingered the paper. "But what do you have for proof? A shoe under a porch? A briefcase that may or may not be buried in the backyard? Not to mention an old guy who was hanging there one minute and gone the next? And you're going to tell them that the neighbors were eating him? I'm not saying I don't believe you. I'm just saying the cops were already there and didn't find anything. So what makes you think they're going to come in, guns blazing, just on your say-so?"

"And it could just piss off Adrien and his mother if I bring the cops sniffing around here again."

"There could be a perfectly logical explanation for everything, you know. Adrien had a dad at one time, I'm sure. Maybe that was his father's stuff."

"Maybe." I toyed with the edge of the paper. "What about the old guy?"

"Really realistic Halloween decoration?" Sam looked at me. "Yeah, I don't think so, either. But without proof . . ."

I sighed. "I know."

"I'll talk to him. Go right over there and tell that loser to quit whatever he's doing. To leave you and Heather alone." Sam leaned toward me and I saw something fierce and protective rise in his face. "When he messes with you two, he's messing with the wrong people."

Sam was no Bruce Willis, but man, it sounded nice to have someone want to take on the world—or just the part next door—to protect me and my sister. "I can handle it."

Sam's hand reached across the table, stopped just beside mine. "You don't have to be brave on your own, Meredith. You have me to help."

I wanted to take his hand, wanted to tell him to stick by my side until this was all done and over. My fingers danced a little on the table, but then I pulled back. Getting Sam involved probably wasn't even fair, especially if this was all some big hallucination. "I think Adrien's just trying to scare me because he knows I don't like him dating Heather. Maybe he and his mother staged that whole thing with the old man. To scare me or something."

Sam considered this for a second. "I don't know, Meredith. I think I should talk to him anyway. Let him know he can't just pull this crap on people."

I stared at his hand for a second. "You don't have to. It's enough that you would."

Sam picked up the paper and turned it toward me. "Maybe. But if Adrien does have anything to do with this guy disappearing, then you're going to need all the help you can get."

"I'll be okay, Sam." I folded the paper up. "It's probably all some big coincidence. Nothing at all to worry about." But I think I was trying to convince myself more than him.

That night, I tried to sleep but couldn't. I tossed and turned, and every time I closed my eyes, I felt as if things were crawling on me. I flailed in the bed, kicking off the sheets, smacking at my skin, but felt nothing other than the sensation of something there.

I fumbled for the light on my nightstand and turned it on. Nothing there. Thank God. I got up, shook out the sheets. Checked under the bed. Still, nothing. I crossed to the picture of my father, sitting now in the frame without any glass. As soon as I picked it up, I swore I smelled the scent of Old Spice again. I inhaled deeply, holding on to the scent for a long time. This time, I felt comforted. As if things were a lot more okay than I had thought.

Either way, I couldn't bring myself to climb back into bed and try to sleep, so I went downstairs. I headed straight for the freezer, emerging with the Ben & Jerry's Chunky Monkey. I grabbed a spoon out of the drawer and ate right out of the carton. Dessert didn't make the feeling of creepy-crawly bugs go away, but it sure as heck made it better.

I sucked down another spoonful of ice cream and crossed to the window. Everything was dark and silent next door. Not a single light burned in the St. Germain windows, except for the light blue glow of the fish tanks. A car came down the street, its headlights sweeping over the house. On the roof, the outline of a tall, skinny bird was illuminated. The vulture. Sitting. Waiting. For what? Me?

I jerked away from the window. I could still feel the bird watching me.

"What are you doing over there, Adrien St. Germain?" I said out loud, to him, to myself.

I dug deeper into my ice cream, trying to unearth a mondo walnut piece buried deep in the middle. This walnut was huge, and I had to carve the spoon around it to dig it out of the banana ice cream. It stuck, frozen in place, and I turned the spoon, trying again—

When the walnut moved. Holy crap.

It moved, honest to God *moved*. It hunched up, backed out of the cavern of ice cream, and swung itself around, becoming not a nut, but a mega cricket or grasshopper, I didn't know, couldn't tell because I was too busy screaming and hucking the entire container of ice cream across the room and into the sink. The pint hit the stainless steel with a thud. Then there was nothing. No sound. No scratching of a bug climbing out. After ten minutes of shaking, I cautiously peered into the sink. Just a spreading pool of pale yellow ice cream with dark brown chunks. Nothing more.

Damn. I'd imagined the whole thing. And wasted my B&J's.

I *must* have imagined it, must have still been freaked out about the bug thing in class. Now I was seeing bugs everywhere.

I headed back to the fridge, propped open the door, and let the cold air out while I tried to find something else I wanted to eat. Moved the milk, shoved some unrecognizable leftovers to the side, pushed the celery my mother always bought and no one ever ate to the right—and found exactly *nada* in interesting consumables. I started to shut the door when I heard—

Laughter. It began low, like a hum, then gradually got louder, as if someone had turned up the volume on a radio. I jerked away from the fridge, slamming the door so hard, the mayo body-slammed the ketchup. I spun around in the kitchen. "Heather? You up?"

No answer. Except for more laughter.

The TV? But no, I could see it from here, and it was off. Neighbors? Windows were closed. Sidewalk empty. Everyone's lights off, people in bed asleep. No one around. What the heck? I must be hearing things. Great. As if I wasn't crazy enough, now I was hearing people who weren't there? My gaze went to the phone. A little white card sat beside it. Dr. Feelgood, ready to take me in and let me talk my fool head off about all this craziness, anytime I wanted.

Maybe it was time to make an appointment. I was clearly a mess.

CHAPTER 23

Heather waited for him, anticipation beating like a jack-hammer in her chest. She shivered and drew her sweatshirt tighter. Not from the cold—it was still so impossibly warm out, she felt as if she were living in the tropics—but from the thick, heavy blackness of night that enveloped her as she huddled against the side of her house.

She glanced up at the windows, but all of them were dark. Good. No one was going to come out here and hassle her again.

"Heather?" Adrien's voice, soft and low, came out of the dark.

She jumped, then turned toward the sound. "Adrien! You scared me!"

"Sorry."

He had come, just as he'd promised after school when

he'd asked her to meet him outside tonight. Joy erupted in Heather's chest. "Geez, I can't believe you don't run into something walking around in the dark with sunglasses on."

"I see very well in the dark." A flash of white as a smile whipped across his face.

"You must eat all your vegetables." Heather laughed. Adrien didn't. Yet another joke he didn't get. Maybe she was just bad at telling them.

"Tell me, Heather," Adrien said, taking her arm, leading her away from the house and out into the night, "tell me what is bothering you. Making you so sad."

She shook her head.

His hand clasped hers. His skin was cold, almost clammy. Was he getting sick, maybe? It was hotter than heck outside, so he couldn't be cold. She wanted to ask, but then he turned his face so he seemed to be looking down at her, and for the first time, Heather felt as though someone was listening. And wasn't going to turn away.

In fact, she could hear it in her head, almost as if Adrien was talking to her. *I'm here, Heather. I always will be. Let me into your heart, your world.*

"Tell me, Heather," he said.

"It's my family." She sighed. "They hate you. And hate us being together even more."

His jaw twitched. "They do?"

She nodded. "My cousins—you know, the twins? They keep saying they're going to come over here and beat you up. I just . . . I . . ." She let out a breath. "I don't want you to get hurt."

"I won't. You don't have to worry."

They veered off the sidewalk, ducking down the alley that ran between the rows of houses. Heather wished the sun would never come up so she could keep on walking with Adrien like this forever. "I will, all the same."

Again that smile, followed by a squeeze of her hand. "And I will worry about you. Now, why don't you tell me what's really bothering you. Why you have that . . . cloak of sadness hanging so heavily over you."

He didn't want to hear that. Didn't want to hear about how she'd screwed up her own family. He was just being nice. She shook her head. "Adrien . . ."

He pulled her into his chest. "I want to know everything about you, Heather. Everything."

I won't judge. I just want to be here for you. I care about you.

She took a deep breath and began to tell him, starting with getting in the car that day, taking a turn too fast, her cell phone sliding off the seat and onto the floor, her reaching for it and unconsciously steering into the opposite lane just as her father shouted at her to watch out, but it was too late, far too late. A sickening crash, a deafening crunch of metal, and then it was over.

When she was done, she was in Adrien's arms, crying, and he was stroking her hair and peppering kisses across her forehead, telling her she was just fine. That he was going to take care of her and make her forget the terrible things that had happened. Make her forget them forever. "Stay with me, Heather, and you'll be happy. Always."

She looked up at him, into eyes she couldn't see, but eyes she trusted all the same, because they seemed to see a part of her no one else had in a long, long time. "Yes, Adrien. I want that. More than you know."

The old woman had been easy to break the other day. She'd come over to bring them muffins, and within minutes, Adrien had had her in the house and under his spell. There would be no more trouble from her.

But her sons—

They'd shown up today, telling Adrien they were going to beat him up. That they didn't like the way he was talking to the girls at school. Adrien had almost laughed and shut the door in their pathetic faces, but then he'd reconsidered and seen the wisdom in convincing them to cooperate. For a week, these two had been a constant thorn in Adrien's side. Now he was about to remove that thorn once and for all.

It had taken some arguing, but finally Adrien had convinced Marie that his way was better. Safer.

Less dangerous than devouring the neighbors and leading suspicion right to their doorstep. He couldn't afford that, not when he was so close to having everything he ever wanted. For now, though, he was going to take care of the one obstacle between himself and Heather.

Her family.

He'd managed to get the boys to come down to the cellar, where they must have thought they could beat him up in private. But Adrien had other ideas.

The twins had been down there for two hours already. He'd thought they'd have given up sooner, but they were stubborn. As he descended the stairs into the cellar, he heard sobbing coming from the second of the boxes.

His smile widened. Finally. The other one had broken.

He enjoyed a challenge. One who didn't give in at the slightest pressure. This one had required so much more. First, Adrien had brought in the bugs. Let them crawl up and down the boy's skin until he'd begged for mercy, his body slick with his own sweat and fluids. But as soon as the bugs were gone, he'd gone back to being defiant. Adrien had gagged him, set him in a corner, then let him watch his brother break, the weaker of the two caving like a robin's egg.

Still, he'd fought Adrien. And so, they'd moved on to the box. An hour inside it, and now the fear emanated off him like cheap cologne.

Leaving the lights off, Adrien crossed to the pine box. As he walked, bugs and spiders followed his steps, skittering away from his shoes. The insects were his companions—but also wary friends who knew better than to cross the master.

Adrien pried up the lid of the coffin, nails screeching as they released their hold. The boy screamed and flailed as the top rose, as if he thought he was getting out. Adrien laughed.

"You sicko, let me go! Let me go!" Tears streamed down the boy's face, smudging the dirt into white streaks.

Adrien leaned in, his face inches away. The kid shrank back, pressing himself into the box again. "I'm the sicko? I'll show you sick." Then Adrien removed his sunglasses.

The boy let out a scream. Adrien clamped a hand over his mouth—they couldn't have that kind of noise, not with the yellow house so close—and leaned in more, narrowing the gap between them, inhaling the boy's fear, tasting it on his tongue, savoring it, until the boy could see everything. See the death that awaited him if he chose to resist anymore.

"I'm going to beat you, you loser!" The boy kicked. He fought. He clawed at Adrien's hand. But he didn't take his eyes away, and slowly, the fight in him began to give way.

Like all the others, he was mesmerized, caught in the twisting, crawling movements of the albino worms. The hissing of the tiny cockroaches. And most of all, buried deepest inside Adrien, the whispers of the souls of all those who had gone before, whistling out of him in a constant, creaky wind.

"You will not fight us anymore," Adrien said, his voice low, slow, measured. "You will help me."

The boy squirmed, tried to free himself.

Adrien's mind reached out to the boy's now weakened mind, sneaking into those vulnerable crevices. *You will obey me. You work for me now. No more fighting.*

Finally, the boy's movements slowed. He nodded. Once. Twice. A third time.

And you will help me when it's time?

The boy nodded again, a tear slipping down his face. It was done. Such a weak creature, considering his youth and brawn. Laughable, really. One of these days, Adrien would have a worthy adversary. He wanted to scream from the boredom of battling these pitiful humans. Adrien removed his hand, stroked the back of it against the boy's cheek. The boy whimpered, then pressed his face into Adrien's palm. Completely at Adrien's mercy now. "When the time is right, I will call you. And you will come."

"Yes." The boy nodded. Agreeable. Helpful.

They would help him to make Heather his forever.

CHAPTER 24

Heather stood on the wooden stairs behind a plywood cut-out of a balcony and looked down at Adrien. Though he was still wearing his sunglasses, she could tell he was looking at her. Heather could hardly think. Barely remember her next line. Her pulse beat with one steady drum—*Adrien, Adrien, Adrien.*

He'd caught up with her at the end of the day and, like always, slid her book bag off her shoulder and onto his own. In five seconds, he'd had her telling him about her day, and he'd listened, really listened, just like he had every time they'd talked over the past month. She spent more and more of her days with Adrien, not just at play practice, but walking to and from school, grabbing seconds between classes. Today, she'd found herself telling him things she'd never told anyone else.

How she walked into school and thought about turning

around the second she got here. How she walked into the lunchroom and wanted to run for the nearest door. How every time she heard a whisper, she was sure it was someone talking about what she had done. Then she'd held her breath, sure he'd offer the same load of bull everyone else had. *It's all in your mind; you'll get over it. Just move on. Deal.*

"I know what that's like," Adrien had said, reaching out and connecting with her, not just with his touch on her arm, but with his voice, his smile. "To think that everyone is talking about you. To feel like the different one. The one no one understands."

"Yes. *Exactly.*" She glanced at him again, sure he was kidding. Instead, he'd taken her in his arms and traced the scar that ran down her face, a scar no amount of CoverGirl could completely hide. "Nobody blames you," he said quietly. "And neither should you."

She'd started to cry and hated herself for crying in front of him, but Adrien hadn't cared. He'd pretended like she wasn't even crying at all, and that had made her feel better in a weird way.

"If your father were alive again today," he'd said, "if he came back, what would he say?"

"That he wanted me to be . . . happy." Another tear ran down her face at the thought of seeing her father one more time. Hearing him call her name and hug her again.

Adrien smiled. "Of course he would. And that's all I want for you, too." Then he kissed her forehead. "It'll be okay, Heather. Because now you're not alone." His smile widened so much, it felt as though it wrapped around her. "Now you have me, too. Forever."

Heather had held on to that sentence. Heard it in her heart, tattooed it onto her brain. She had Adrien. She, Heather Willis, the girl who had lost everything. Including her place in the world. But now, with Adrien, she felt as though she finally had it back.

Her life suddenly seemed so unbelievably perfect. This morning at breakfast, Aunt Evelyn had asked about "that nice boy you've been dating." And when the twins had inquired about Adrien's whereabouts, Heather assumed they just wanted to know so they could beat him up, but they surprised her by saying, "No. We are going to see if he wanted to shoot some hoops."

Ted faked making a basket. "Seriously. We're cool with him."

Her jaw dropped. "Really?"

"Really," Tad said. "You should stick with him. He's a good guy. With good intentions."

"Yeah, good intentions," Ted echoed.

Then they both turned toward her at the same time. And smiled. Just like she was smiling now, as she gazed at Adrien.

"Action!" Mr. Edwards called, waving toward the players on the stage.

Adrien moved, stepping into the scene made just for the two of them. The rest of the cast hung back, watching the set crew paint the plywood backing. Heather didn't pay much attention to anyone else, though. She was watching only one person. "'He jests at scars that never felt a wound,'" Adrien said, taking several steps toward the makeshift balcony holding Heather.

She moved closer to the cut-out window and looked down at him, smiling. Romeo. Her Romeo. No one else's. He smiled back. "'But soft! What light through yonder window breaks? It is the east, and Juliet is the sun!'" Adrien said.

"Cut!" Mr. Edwards interrupted. "Adrien, why don't we lose the sunglasses? Let everyone see your eyes. See you emote."

Adrien turned toward Mr. Edwards. "Sir, all due respect to Shakespeare, but we are targeting a younger audience with this masterpiece, are we not?"

Mr. Edwards nodded.

"And to do that, we should take a younger audience approach." He gestured toward his sunglasses and his jacket. "In our dress, our mannerisms, and even, yes, our sunglasses."

Mr. Edwards stared at Adrien for a long minute. "You think wearing sunglasses and dressing like Justin Timberlake will make the play more accessible to the teenagers watching it?"

"Yes, sir, I do."

Mr. Edwards paced for a sec. "You make a good point. All right. We'll try it your way, Adrien. Baz Luhrmann did it in Hollywood; we can do it here at Jefferson. Anything that gets kids in here to hear the words of the immortal Bard is good with me."

The other cast members shouted a relieved "Yeah!" at not having to wear goofy English Tudor or Victorian or whatever stupid era costumes Mr. Edwards had planned. Real clothes meant real comfort. Only Wendell pouted. Knowing him, he probably had a set of tights just waiting at home for a chance to shine on a stage.

"Action," Mr. Edwards called again, gesturing to them to begin again.

Adrien moved back to the starting place and repeated his first few lines. Once again, they soared through Heather's heart. She wasn't Juliet—she was a planet in the Adrien St. Germain orbit. Destined to stay as long as she could.

CHAPTER 25

Heather had stopped talking to me entirely. After the dinner at Adrien's and the whole disappearing-old-man thing, she wouldn't even look at me, never mind say a word. It had been several weeks of silence, and I was sick of it.

I headed into the yearbook office, camera slung over my shoulder, and dropped into the seat beside Sam.

"Did you get the pictures of the cross-country team practice?" he asked.

I shook my head. "I'm really not in the mood for any of this right now."

He shrugged, as if it were no big deal. "Hey, don't forget we're supposed to take pics at the dress rehearsal tonight. I was thinking we should take a few more after the play, too. I'm going to check the layout from last year's book and see what they did with the school play."

I groaned. The last thing I wanted to see in my lens was Adrien making puppy eyes at my sister. My whole family seemed to be on this pro-Adrien kick lately, and it was irritating as hell. Aunt Evelyn had totally gone to the dark side—meaning she was raving on and on about how amazing Adrien was. What a gracious host he'd been. How we needed to return the favor and invite him and his mother over to our house. Same thing with the twins. All of a sudden they were, like, prez and VP of the Adrien fan club. And my mother hadn't been paying attention to anything for the past seven or eight months—what had made me think she'd start now?

Sam reached out and his hand covered mine. A spark ran through me. "It'll be okay, Mer."

"I hope so."

"Has anything else happened?"

"Nope. It's been quiet next door for a couple weeks now." I'd been keeping my distance. Well, as much distance as a next-door neighbor could keep. No more spying trips with Cassidy.

Sam stared at the computer screen for a minute. "They never found that missing guy, you know."

I'd been reading the paper, too, looking for some clue. "I know." Maybe I should call the cops again and this time insist they go through Adrien's house. Somehow, I had a feeling that the results would be the same. That no matter how many times the cops showed up at Adrien's house, he'd find a way to sweet-talk them right on down the driveway.

Sam pushed back from the desk and got to his feet. "Come on, let's get out of here. Go play laser tag or something."

"I can't. I have a doctor's appointment downtown."

"No problem. I'll drive you, and then we can head over to the dress rehearsal together."

"You don't have to, Sam, really. I can catch a bus."

He grinned, and my heart flip-flopped in my chest. "I want to."

And I wanted him to, too. More than I could say. After a few really sucky weeks, things suddenly seemed to have a bright side.

A half hour later, I sat in a stiff armchair across from the psychiatrist I'd seen a few times after my dad died. I didn't want to tell this guy what I'd been seeing, but there was no way I wanted to go home and see bugs in my ice cream again. Maybe if I talked about it, it would stop. So I spilled my guts for, like, twenty minutes.

"This is all normal." Dr. Howard sat back, one leg crossed over the other, wearing a tweed jacket and glasses, as though he'd opened up a catalog of psychiatrist looks and ordered every item.

"Normal?"

"You've experienced an enormous trauma in your life, Meredith. It's a delayed reaction to the tragic events that happened eight months ago." Dr. Howard leaned forward, his little clipboard and pen in his hands. "You didn't grieve then, Meredith. You were the strong one. The one who held everything together."

Tears welled in my eyes, and I shoved the back of my fist against them. "Yeah, well, someone had to stay home from the mall."

He made a little face at my sarcasm. To a doc, that wasn't dealing. To me, it was dealing just fine. "You need to talk about what happened. Talk about your feelings. If you let all that anxiety out, then it won't manifest itself in these . . . visions."

"Visions? Or do you mean hallucinations?"

He shifted in his chair, then made a little note. "I prefer not to use that term."

Probably because it had the Crazy label all over it. "Okay. Whatev."

"Do you think perhaps your Fuchs' has contributed to this?" he asked.

Did everyone have to think that? Why didn't he just believe me? "I saw the eye doc several weeks ago. He said I was fine. I have, like, almost zero symptoms. Just that my eyes get dry sometimes. My dad was the one who had it bad. He couldn't even drive, which was why . . ." I stopped talking. I wasn't going to go there. Didn't need to talk about that today.

Dr. Howard apparently disagreed. "Which was why what?"

I shook my head. "You know this part."

"I know, but I'd like to hear it from you."

I looked at his framed degrees, all hung in a row on the wall. Bachelor's, master's, PhD. Harvard, all of them. Made the guy smart, I supposed. Didn't mean I had to like his questions. "Which was why . . ." I took in a breath, let it out. ". . . my sister was driving . . . that day."

Dr. Howard nodded. Waited for me to go on. I didn't.

He made a face, then a note on his pad of paper. Whatever test he'd given me, I'd probably failed. I didn't care. I wasn't here to talk about me and Heather. I was here so he'd make the seeing-bugs-and-men-hanging-in-the-neighbor's-cellar "visions" stop.

"Well, if you continue to see these . . . things, I want you to come and see me more frequently." He opened up his appointment book, scanned the pages, then wrote down something on a little card and handed it to me. "For now, let's stick to twice a week. How does that sound?"

Like complete torture. Why had I thought this was a good idea? Maybe Dr. Howard was right, though. Maybe just telling him would make whatever it was that I was seeing go away. I took the card and pocketed it. "Sure."

He nodded. It said he had heard all this before and much, much worse. "Say hello to your mother and sister for me, Meredith. And tell them they can come see me anytime, too."

"Yeah. I'll do that."

Then I left. Cured.

Or so I thought.

The high school was quiet—everyone had gone home, except the band, which was practicing in the band room and let out an off-tune screech every once in a while, and the cast and crew of the play, still there for the dress rehearsal. Our shoes echoed on the tile as we walked down the hall and toward the yearbook office to get the camera. "So, you never answered my question the other day," Sam said.

"What question?"

He stopped walking. "Are we? Just friends?"

Had he been thinking about that question as much as I had in the past several weeks? "Well, uh, we should be. I mean, you and Heather . . ."

Sam unlocked the door to the yearbook office and we stepped inside. The camera sat on the shelf, but neither one of us grabbed it. "Me and Heather what? She's dating Adrien."

I touched his shoulder. Like a friend, even if what I felt for him was more than friendly. "That's got to be hard for you. But trust me, you're the boyfriend every girl wishes she had."

"Oh, yeah?" He let out a half laugh. "Then why is Adrien the one every girl in school is killing to get?"

"Not *every* girl in this school wants Adrien," I said quietly. I held his gaze for a second longer, and then I looked down and studied the ugly green tile floor. I was acutely aware that we were totally alone in the tiny yearbook office.

He put a finger under my chin and lifted it up. "Oh, yeah? Who are you interested in, Meredith?"

Oh. Boy. How was I supposed to answer that question? I took the chicken route and didn't say anything at all, just stood there with his finger under my chin, staring helplessly at the guy I shouldn't want but did anyway.

A smile took over Sam's face. One I'd never seen before. One I really, really liked. A lot. Then he leaned forward, in super slow mo—

And kissed me.

CHAPTER 26

Heather could have been in a dream, except she knew this was real. The last dress rehearsal before tonight's performance. And then, tomorrow, the play would be done and she would stop being Juliet, Adrien would be done playing Romeo. Tonight, she decided, she'd enjoy every second. She stood across from Adrien on the stage and actually felt as if she really were Juliet. Adrien said Romeo's words, and they sang across Heather's heart. Did he really mean them? Or was he just that good of an actor?

He moved closer, took her hand. She wished she could see past his sunglasses, to read the thoughts in his eyes. But now that Mr. Edwards had agreed to take the R&J production up a modern notch, the sunglasses—which she'd never actually seen Adrien without—and Adrien's A&F jacket collection had stayed. Regardless, he looked like every girl's dream Romeo.

The best part? He was *Heather's* Romeo.

"'My name, dear saint, is hateful to myself,'" Adrien was saying, and Heather drew herself back to the scene, to the Shakespearean wording, "'Because it is an enemy to thee. Had I it written, I would tear the word.'"

Something flickered across his face, a muscle ticking in his jaw, when he stopped talking, as if he felt the words, too. She reached for him, her hand landing on his, and delivered her lines, ending with "'Art thou not Romeo, and a Montague?'"

"'Neither, fair maid, if either thee dislike.'" His fingers tightened around hers. In her head, she heard him whisper, *Please don't judge me on who I am. Just on who I want to be.*

They went forward with the next few lines, where she warned him that her family was out to kill him and he talked about how his life would be better even with them hating him than if he'd never met her at all. Even though he was speaking lines written hundreds of years ago by someone else, it all sounded so *real,* as if Adrien were speaking right from his heart. As though this battle to be accepted by her family was exactly the same today for him as it had been for Romeo. Every time he touched her, she heard the echo of his voice in her head.

"'What satisfaction canst thou have tonight?'" she asked her Romeo, wishing they were alone. That there was no one watching them act this scene out.

"'Th' exchange of thy love's faithful vow for mine.'" Adrien dropped to one knee on the platform beside the balcony, then put a hand out to hers. As if he was . . . proposing.

Marriage. Adrien was talking about marriage.

No, no, get a grip, Heather, she told herself. *Romeo* was talking to *Juliet* about marriage.

But even though they'd rehearsed this scene many times before, the significance of the lines hit her.

"'I gave thee mine before thou didst request it,'" she whispered, realizing as the line left her that she'd just said yes. No, Juliet had, she reminded herself again. Except it all felt so *real,* as if Adrien were talking just to her.

"Excellent, excellent," Mr. Edwards cut in. "But I'd like to try it again, this time with a little less of a shell-shocked reaction from you, Heather. Remember, back in those days, it was customary for girls younger than you to get married. So she won't have that deer-in-headlights look when Romeo proposes."

"Okay," Heather said, then took a few steps back to return to her original position. Adrien did the same. They started the scene over, and once again, he moved forward and took her hand.

This time, Heather allowed the words to sink in, to become real. Not as if she were Juliet, but as if she, Heather Willis, were actually getting married to Adrien St. Germain. In her head, she heard him say, *Marry me, Heather. Say you'll be mine forever.*

"Yes," she whispered, the word a breath, then caught herself and remembered the lines. "And . . . 'And all my fortunes at thy foot I'll lay And follow thee my lord throughout the world.'"

Adrien smiled, then reached up, cupping her jaw. He closed the distance between them and brought his mouth to her ear. "I mean it. I would love to marry you . . . for real," he whispered.

"Romeo, 'tis—"

"You, Heather. Not Juliet."

Her eyes widened, and she stumbled in place. She hadn't been imagining it at all. He did mean every word. "You . . . you . . . what?"

He nodded, his thumb caressing the tender skin of her jaw. She couldn't think, couldn't do anything but concentrate on his touch. The words he'd said, the rapid beating of her heart.

Mr. Edwards let out a large sigh. "Shock again. Heather, Heather, Heather. Remember, Juliet is not surprised to hear this. Perhaps, yes, it's a little sudden because—"

"She barely knows him," Heather finished.

"Yes, yes. But in that time, she has fallen—"

"Deeply in love," Heather finished again, her gaze never leaving Adrien's face. His smile widened, as slow as molasses, and he nodded. Agreeing.

"Absolutely," Mr. Edwards said, pleased because he thought they were reading into the play, not each other, "and so her answer to his proposal will be an easy, fast—"

"Yes," Heather said, knowing the whole idea was insane— she was a junior in high school, for Pete's sake, but surely Adrien didn't mean now. "Yes, yes, yes."

He moved in closer. *This was it,* she thought. The moment she had waited for, for so, so long. Heather gazed down at Adrien's perfect lips and her heart started beating faster. She inhaled and caught the scent of his cologne. Something earthy, woodsy. It was so . . . irresistible. Left her begging for more, to touch him, to trail kisses along his neck and inhale again. To just stay wrapped up in his arms forever and ever and ever.

"Heather," he whispered, his cool breath dancing across her face. Suddenly she felt as though time had stopped. As if they were the only people in the world.

Adrien St. Germain was going to kiss her. No, her *fiancé* was going to kiss her. And it would be so amazing, so wonderful, everything she had dreamed.

She leaned forward across the balcony, closing her eyes, waiting for that exquisite moment when Adrien's lips would meet hers and their promise would be sealed—

"All righty, people, that was great!" Mr. Edwards exclaimed. "Adrien, Heather, I could really feel the intensity! You almost had me believing you were engaged." He let out a laugh. "Okay, everyone, don't forget to be back here by five o'clock to get ready for opening night."

Adrien stepped back, the moment over. Any chance of a kiss totally gone. Bummer. Disappointment sat heavy in Heather's stomach.

People left the area, and Heather climbed out of the balcony, meeting Adrien on the stage. The auditorium emptied out pretty fast, and before she knew it, only she and Adrien were left behind.

"Do you regret it?" he asked her.

"Regret what?"

"Getting engaged." He smiled. "Promising to marry me. To be with me forever."

He really had meant it. Oh, God, it was a crazy idea. She was just sixteen. But surely he didn't mean they'd get married, like, now. Either way, to think that Adrien St. Germain wanted to marry her, of all the girls in this school—

The thought took the breath right out of her chest.

"No, Adrien, I don't regret it at all," she said. "I'd love . . . to marry you."

The smile that crossed his face this time was bigger than any she'd seen before. He climbed up and into the balcony, then drew her to him, bringing her cheek to his chest. "Good. Because being with you for eternity would make me happier than anything else in the world."

"You're what? Marrying him? Oh my God, Heather, are you freaking *insane?*" Meredith's outraged voice cut through the auditorium and sliced the edge off Heather's joy.

But before Heather could turn around and argue with her sister, she heard the slam of the auditorium door. It echoed and echoed all through the empty space.

CHAPTER 27

I ran. I ran until my lungs gave out and my legs were on fire. Until I stopped, I hadn't even realized I had had a destination. Then I saw the tall, curved wrought-iron gates of the Parkwood Cemetery looming before me, and I knew this was where I'd meant to come all along. Probably from the first day everything had started to go so horribly wrong.

I pushed through the gates and plunged into the cemetery, tears blurring my vision. It didn't matter. I knew the route by heart, had been here so often in the first few months that I could tell someone exactly how many steps it was from the main gate to the headstone.

Four hundred and seventy-three.

The sun was starting to set, and the cemetery was completely in the shade, cast in shadows. There weren't any lights in here, except for the few by the front gates. Maybe they figured no one came into a cemetery after dark, or maybe they were just too cheap to install them. I charged up the hill, my lungs straining to keep up with the effort, and finally stopped in front of the curved granite marker.

ROBERT WILLIS, it read. BELOVED HUSBAND AND FATHER.

I dropped to the ground, collapsing into the soft grass. "How could you?" My fists pounded into the ground, denting the manicured lawn. "How could you leave us?"

There was no answer. I hadn't expected one. But still, I desperately wished I could hear my father's voice one more time, hear him give me some kind of advice, something to deal with this mess my life had become. I'd been smelling his cologne, looking at his picture, but it wasn't enough. It wasn't him. Loneliness and helplessness swamped me.

"We need you, Dad," I cried, and then his name slipped from Dad to Daddy as the tears poured out of me, and I hung on his headstone, just like I used to hang on him when I was little. But the rock was cold and unyielding and didn't hug me back. "Oh, Daddy, *I* need you. Heather's a mess, Mom's never home, and you're . . ." A sob ripped out of my throat, and I hugged the hard stone, wishing it were my father instead. "You're *not here.*"

Silence. Nothing. No dad, no answers. Pain ripped through me. I pounded at the stone, slamming my fists into the granite until my hands hurt, but it didn't change anything. Didn't bring me answers, or bring my father back. I wiped away my tears and sat back on my heels.

That was when I noticed the gravesites around me.

It felt as though it was getting darker by the second, but even in the waning light, I could see several yawning holes, looking as if some gopher had gone on a rampage. Not just one or two, or even three, but a dozen, maybe two dozen, of the gravesites ripped open, the earth thrown to the side, the caskets brought to the surface, tossed haphazardly onto the ground.

The lids were removed. Flung to the side, as if someone had been in a real hurry to open those caskets.

What on earth? Why? What reason could anyone possibly have for doing something like that? I stood and crossed to the closest gravesite, my steps slow, my heart slamming in my chest. I didn't want to look. Didn't want to know. But I had to. I closed my eyes, then bent forward and looked inside the nearest open casket.

Nothing. The casket was empty. The putrid smell of decay wafted out of the pit, making me gag. I backed up quickly.

In a way, it was a relief not to see a corpse, but in another way, it scared the crap out of me. I mean, where was the body? It didn't just walk away. It had to be here somewhere.

I wished I had grabbed Sam before I'd left the school, but he'd been on the computer in the yearbook office and my only thought after seeing my sister and Adrien had been to get out of there.

I ran to the next casket. Same as the first. Empty. So was the next one I checked. And the one after that. And the one after that. Every grave I could see around me had been opened up—but had no corpse inside. Someone had taken the bodies. Why? And to where?

It couldn't have been an animal. To do that much damage, it would have taken Bigfoot and all his friends. I thought of grave robbers, but it wasn't as though our town held the bodies of the Rockefellers or as if anyone here was likely to be buried draped in diamonds or something.

I stood in the cemetery and did a slow turn. Who would do something like this? And where were the dead people?

The answer came to me in an instant. Cold and hard, like a punch to my gut. Impossible, I told myself. That was the kind of stuff I read about, saw in horror movies, but sure as hell didn't see in real life. But as I turned again and saw empty grave after empty grave, then looked down and, in the last whispers of light, saw the unmistakable indents of handprints in the freshly turned earth and, incredibly, *footprints* leading away from the graves . . .

There was no other conclusion. What else could climb out of a grave and walk away?

Zombies.

Oh my God. Even as I told myself it was impossible, that those things were fictional, only in movies, I saw dozens and dozens of footprints merging together into one path that led from the graves and out of the cemetery.

Zombies? Honest to God, walking dead?

I stumbled back, nearly falling into one of the holes myself, then turned and ran, even though my legs already hurt and my lungs were screaming at me to walk. I burst through the cemetery gates. Thinking I'd escaped. Not so sure I had.

CHAPTER 28

Marie was gone.

Adrien's fury rose and exploded in a fist that went through the wall. The sheetrock imploded, the hole so wide and deep that it punched through to the next room in a flattened circle. Another fist, another hole, but still the fury bubbled inside him, an unstoppable wave.

Gone? Where would she go? Hunting again?

No. The vulture still sat on the roof, the crows still lined the ridges. He sensed the hyenas waiting somewhere far away. They had not followed her. So wherever Marie had gone, it hadn't been with the intention of hunting for a meal. That meant she had had some other task in mind. Something she hadn't shared. Marie was keeping a secret, and Adrien didn't like that. At all.

He needed her here. Now.

Marie had never given him the Knowledge after that dinner with Heather's family, as she had promised. And Adrian had retaliated by refusing to hunt for her. She must be wild with hunger. She couldn't possibly refuse him now.

Heather was sitting in the car, lured here after the dress rehearsal by his promise of a "surprise." It was the gift he'd waited to give her for so, so long.

Heather had agreed to be his forever—and that meant he needed the Knowledge, needed to turn her into a zombie like him. If he didn't do it now, he could lose his chance. What if she changed her mind? He'd worked so hard to get to this point, to bring Heather to him willingly. And now that he had her, Marie had broken their agreement and abandoned him?

For what? To go where? And do what?

Unease settled inside him. She was up to something, something bad. Whatever it was, Adrien did not intend to let her continue. He was the one in charge, the stronger one. Marie had no hope in a battle against him.

He left the house. He paused, sniffing the air. She hadn't gone far. He would find her—

And when he did, he would rip the Knowledge from her, one bite at a time. Marie would learn her lesson for toying with him.

CHAPTER 29

Heather wanted to tell someone—anyone.

She was engaged to Adrien St. Germain. He loved her, wanted to marry her. Be with her forever. The thought was almost too big to hold inside herself.

But she had to. For one, Adrien hadn't said whether he wanted their engagement to be public knowledge. And for another, even though most of her family seemed okay with Adrien now, chances were, if she told them, they'd all freak and do something stupid like call the cops or get a restraining order or something. That was the last thing she needed.

Maybe that was why Adrien had told her, after the proposal, that they had to make a quick trip home. He'd said he had a surprise for her. Was it some way of telling everyone about their engagement? Or was it something special for her?

She couldn't wait to find out. She sat in the passenger's seat of his red Camaro, anxiously waiting for Adrien to return. She didn't even want to go into her house, for fear she would blurt out, "Adrien and I are engaged," to one of her family members. Clearly Meredith hadn't taken the news too well.

A familiar car pulled up in front of her house. Sam's car.

"Hey, Heather," he said as he strode up Adrien's driveway. She rolled down the window so he could talk to her. "Have you seen Meredith?"

"No," Heather said. She glanced again at Adrien's house. She hoped he didn't take long getting her surprise. "I don't know where she is. She just went running out of the school."

"I know, one of the crew members told me they saw her leaving. They said she was in tears. Any idea what got her so upset?"

Heather shrugged nonchalantly. She wasn't going to tell Sam about her and Adrien. That was all she needed right now, another person freaking out about her life.

"Hey," Sam said, "what are you doing here, anyway? Aren't you supposed to be at the school getting ready for the big show tonight?"

"I'm going back there soon," Heather said. "But, um, something came up and Adrien and I had to stop back here first."

Sam made a face. "Of course. Adrien. Don't you think maybe you and he are moving kinda fast?" he said. "I, uh, saw your Facebook update."

For a second there, Heather panicked, thinking Sam knew about the engagement. Then she realized it was just the "I'm in love" thing she'd posted the other day that had him all weirded out. How could that be bad? Kids posted that kind of thing all the time. Heather was saved from an uncomfortable conversation with Sam when she heard a soft rustle on the grass. She turned, and Adrien was standing there. Smiling.

Heather got out of the car. Adrien closed the distance between them in an instant. "Heather. Finally." He reached for her and grabbed her hand. His hair was mussed, his shirt was untucked, and he looked . . . worried. *You're here, you're here. Thank goodness.*

Even a mess, he was still the most handsome boy she'd ever seen. "Do you have my surprise ready?"

"Soon, very soon."

"I can't wait."

His smile echoed hers. "Neither can I."

Adrien noticed Sam there and looked at him questioningly. "He's just here looking for Meredith," Heather explained.

A quick frown appeared on Adrien's face, and then it disappeared. "Meredith's not home," he said. "She went to visit a friend."

Sam eyed him. "How do you know? She wouldn't tell you. She doesn't even like you."

"People change their mind about me all the time." Adrien took a step closer to Sam, releasing Heather as he did. "And you—friend, boyfriend, whatever you are—you could, too."

Sam snorted. "That I doubt."

"Never doubt the power of a few minutes of . . . conversation."

Sam closed in on Adrien and pointed a finger at his chest. "I don't want a conversation with you. Not today, not tomorrow, not ever. So don't be trying to make friends with me, dude."

"Sam!" Heather wanted to hit him. Never had she seen him be so mean to anyone before. "Stop. Seriously. Get out of here!"

Sam looked at Adrien, then back at Heather. "I'm going to look for Meredith. *Somebody* should worry about her." Then he got into his car and left.

"I'm so, so sorry," Heather said after Sam was gone. "I don't know what got into him."

Adrien reached up and cupped her jaw, his touch so tender, Heather wanted to melt. "There will always be people who are against us, my love. We have to be stronger than them. More determined to be together." His sunglassed gaze met hers. "Are you willing to do whatever it takes to be with me?"

"Yes," she said. "Anything."

He smiled. "Then trust me. The surprise isn't quite ready yet. I thought it would be by the time you got here, but I need more . . . time. Will you wait for me?"

"Of course."

"I won't be gone long." He touched her hand, and she shivered.

Soon, so soon, my sweet. We'll be together. Forever.

"Good," she said, then offered up a smile of her own.

He pressed a kiss to her forehead—God, why didn't he just kiss her for real, already? Was that part of the surprise?— then got into his car and took off, peeling out of the driveway in a screech of rubber.

After Adrien left, Heather stood outside her house and debated going inside. She saw her mother's car in the driveway and a light on in the twins' room.

"Heather?"

She turned. She saw someone standing in the shadows outside of Adrien's house but couldn't see who it was. Heather took a few steps closer. "Mrs. St. Germain?"

"Yes," the woman said, the *s* at the end of the word seeming to carry on and on. "And please, call me Marie." Her hand reached out from the shadows and beckoned to Heather. "Won't you come over here and meet me?"

A shiver chased up Heather's spine. She couldn't have said why. This was Adrien's mother. No one to worry about. Then why did she hesitate before crossing the distance between their two yards? Why did she feel, just for a second, as if Adrien was whispering in her head, *Don't go with her, don't trust her*?

Heather shrugged off the feelings. Then she crossed the yard and put her hand into Marie's. It wasn't until Marie's cold, rough fingers closed over Heather's with a vicelike grip that she realized she'd made a mistake.

A horrible, horrible mistake.

CHAPTER 30

I ran out of the cemetery, burst through the gates, and ran all the way home.

"What's wrong?" Aunt Evelyn asked as I stood there panting in the kitchen.

"The cemetery . . . it . . . the graves . . ." I couldn't get a sentence out, couldn't make words string together. "So many . . . oh my God."

Mom, home for once, looked up from her coffee. "Meredith, what happened?"

"I went . . ." I took in a breath. Another. "I went to the cemetery to visit Dad and I saw them."

"Saw what?"

"The graves, they were all open. All dug up."

My mother waved that off and went back to her coffee.

"They're moving part of the cemetery, remember? To make way for condos."

"But what if—"

"The units should be ready by the spring," my mother continued. "They should bring me some good commissions."

It made sense, and now that she said it, I remembered hearing something about the cemetery being moved. But I had thought that plan was months, maybe even years, off, though. And when I thought of those uprooted graves . . .

Something didn't add up.

Besides, why would any developer move a cemetery like that? Just tear the place apart?

"Evelyn, are you almost ready to go?" my mom asked. She crossed to the sink, dumped out the rest of her coffee, and put the mug in the dishwasher. "I want to stop at the florist, too, before the play starts."

The play. I didn't want to go but told myself that maybe it would take my mind off everything for a little while. I glanced outside and realized I didn't see the Tweedle Twins anywhere. "Are Ted and Tad going to the play?"

Aunt Evelyn nodded. "My boys have volunteered to be ushers tonight. As a tribute to Heather and Adrien." Aunt Evelyn gave me a small smile. "Isn't it wonderful she's going out with Adrien? He's a nice boy and he makes her so happy."

Something didn't seem right about Aunt Evelyn. "You feeling all right, Aunt Evelyn?"

"Just fine, just fine." She smiled again, then grabbed her purse from the counter. "I need to get to the grocery store first thing in the morning. I want to cook a special dinner for tomorrow, when I invite over Adrien and his mother."

"Why on earth would we have them over for dinner?" I asked. I glanced at my mother, who just shrugged.

"Why, to celebrate, of course." Aunt Evelyn smiled for a third time, then walked out the door, humming.

The song?

"Chapel of Love." You know, that oldies song about going to the chapel and getting "ma-a-a-arried."

Even my aunt was behind this marriage thing to the freak next door? What was going on?

"Do you want to join us or do you have your own ride?" my mom asked as she headed out.

I paced the kitchen. What was I going to do? No one believed me about Adrien.

I glanced out the window. The red Camaro wasn't in its usual place in the driveway next door. I told myself that was because Adrien hadn't gone home between dress rehearsal and the performance, but the more I looked at that empty space, the more I got the feeling something was wrong. "You and Aunt Evelyn can go," I said. "I have something I have to do first."

As soon as they were gone, I decided I would go next door, telling myself I felt a lot braver than I did. One way or another, I was going to get some answers. Because there was no way—no way in hell—I was letting my sister marry that freak.

But first I decided I'd call my sister herself. Get some answers from her. Finally.

CHAPTER 31

After leaving Heather, Adrien drove up and down the streets, searching for an hour, aware of the ticking clock. The hyenas were out looking for Marie; the vulture circled lazily above him doing the same. Why couldn't they find her? Where could she have gone that his spies would miss? He was already supposed to be at the school, and if he didn't show up, he knew Heather would be upset. Surely she had gone ahead to get ready for the play.

He sensed Marie, caught her scent several times, and knew she had to be just ahead of him. She wasn't smart enough or fast enough to avoid him forever, nor was she strong enough to hunt for anything substantial, so he finally gave up and returned to the house. And there she was, sitting in the darkness, in a chair on the porch, like a starving dog forced to return to its abusive master for a scrap of meat.

Marie was falling apart. Her skin peeled off in chunks, her face drooped heavily on one side, her fingers had fallen off and had been reattached with Super Glue. She needed a new body. Desperately. Adrien stood over her. "I want the Knowledge. Now."

Marie shook her head, and a hunk of her dark brown hair tumbled to the floor. "No. I've heard about your plan. You're going to marry that girl. Keep her."

Damn. How had she found out? His desire was overpowering his better sense. "I want her, Marie. And you won't stop me."

"You don't choose who gets raised and who doesn't. Only the one with the Knowledge does." A crafty smile curved across her face. "And that one is me."

He roared back at her, "Who are you to tell me what I can do? I want her and I will have her. I will not walk this earth for the next millennia alone."

"It makes you vulnerable," she whispered. "Weaker."

"That is where you are wrong. I will be stronger with Heather beside me." *And without you,* he wanted to add. But he didn't. He would eliminate Marie when he was ready. After he had what he wanted. Unfortunately, until then, he needed to keep this worthless drag on his plans.

"And now, I'm going to make sure you don't do something stupid."

Something in Marie's voice, some low, guttural tone, raised an alarm in Adrien. "What do you mean, you're going to make sure?"

"I have her. And I'm going to keep her."

Alarm bells clanged in his head. *I have her.* His confidence faltered. "What . . . what are you talking about?"

"Don't worry, she's safe. For now." Marie laughed. "She's being kept somewhere far from here. When the time is right, I will take her body and make it my own."

Adrien lunged for Marie, his hands closing around her throat. "You let her go. Now."

Even as her eyes bulged above his tightening grip, Marie smiled, a smile that had only a couple of teeth left in it. "You're not in charge anymore, Adrien," she managed to say. "You never really were. And now, I must go. Because I have plans, for her and for everyone else in this ridiculous town."

Then she rose and threw his hand off her neck. Before he could react, she pushed past him with a strength that surprised him. She raised a finger, and then several figures emerged from the shadows of the porch, surrounding Adrien in a tight, inescapable circle.

Telling Adrien that he had seriously miscalculated Marie's will to survive.

CHAPTER 32

Heather didn't answer her cell. Every time I got her voice mail, my heart stopped. I told myself she was busy with the play, that she was backstage, phone off. But every time I looked at that empty driveway next door, I knew she was with him.

Adrien pulled into the driveway. His car's engine rumbled for a second, and then he shut it off. He stopped on the porch.

Alone. Where was my sister? Only one way to find out, I decided. And I wanted to confront him about that proposal. What was he thinking, getting engaged to a sixteen-year-old girl? He was using her, I was sure of it, and I was going to make sure Adrien knew there was no way I was going to let that happen.

I skulked along Adrien's house, pausing by the basement windows, but it was dark in the cellar and getting dark outside and I couldn't see anything. I crawled over to the window that had been curtainless before. They'd replaced the black cloth, but still a corner drooped.

I reached forward, trying to rub the dirt off the glass, when I was yanked to my feet. A cold, scaly hand went over my mouth and I was dragged back, my heels digging into the ground.

I fought, kicking out my arms and legs, but whoever had me was ridiculously strong and determined. It didn't speak, just dragged me away from the window and around to the back door of Adrien's house. The door opened and I was shoved inside. Into the darkness.

"Welcome, Meredith," a rough, gravelly female voice said. "You've been so curious about what we do here. It's time I showed you."

My eyes adjusted to the dark interior, and as they did, the woman's face came into a dim focus. Adrien's mother. Only now she looked so much worse than when I'd seen her in the basement, like someone who was dying. Or worse . . . already dead?

Her skin, what was left of it, was as pale as a sheet. The rest had fallen off, revealing part of her skull and some bones. A few strands of brown hair stuck out in clumps, bald spots peppering her scalp. Her mouth drooped to one side, and drool spilled out of her lips, puddling at her feet. Every part of her seemed to be peeling, rotting, falling apart. The worst part was the smell. It hit me in a wave of rot, as though a garbage truck had overturned in front of me. I gagged, trying to keep my stomach from upchucking. God. What was wrong with her?

Was she . . . oh God, one of them? The walking dead?

I tried to back up, to get out, but whoever had grabbed me was still there, a wall behind me. I tried to turn, but strong arms grasped mine. I looked down and let out a scream. Those weren't hands on my arms. They were skeleton fingers. I finally was able to turn my head and saw a corpse grinning at me as he shoved me closer to that woman thing.

Adrien's mother smiled, a long slow smile that curved up her face, until her jaw dropped open and I could see inside her mouth.

Into a yawning, empty black cavity. No teeth. No tongue. Nothing but black . . .

Hell.

"You're not going anywhere, Meredith," Adrien's mother said. Then she waved at the thing behind me. "Take her to the cellar. And don't eat her before I say you can."

Eat me? No, no, *no.*

I opened my mouth to scream, but it was too late. The zombie put a raggedy, bony hand over my lips, sending dirt and bugs down my throat. The only sound I heard as I was dragged down the wooden cellar stairs was the woman's laughter.

CHAPTER 33

Adrien's plan was falling apart and he needed to find a way to get it back together. Now. Before he lost Heather and lost everything that mattered. Marie said she had her, but *where* was the bigger question. He didn't sense Heather in the house, and that meant Marie had taken her somewhere else. Where?

And worse, he'd been imprisoned by those morons working for Marie. Inside his worst nightmare. A coffin.

He forced himself to stay calm. To hold on to a memory of Heather, because it was the only thing keeping him sane as the wooden walls seemed to close in on him, pressing down and in. He pushed at the sides, pressed his feet into the base. Not a millimeter of movement. Of course—Adrien had built these himself, and he'd built them well. Somehow, he had to get out of here before he went insane. Or worse, before he was buried alive.

He heard the cellar door open, and then the heavy, dull footsteps of a zombie headed into the basement. Above the scent of death, he caught another scent, a familiar one. Meredith.

Marie had captured the sister? Adrien shifted in the coffin—oh, how Marie would pay for this later, knowing full well that his deepest fear was being placed in the ground alive—and evaluated this new circumstance. Good . . . or bad?

Good, he decided. The sister would be a distraction for Marie, one way or another. And for him, that meant an opportunity. He shoved at the lid on the coffin, but it stuck, both nailed shut and secured with padlocks. Panic seized him, and he fought to keep himself from bucking at the wooden box and letting Marie know she was winning.

Adrien stilled himself. And concentrated. There had to be another way out of this prison.

He heard the jangle of chains, the muffled screams of Meredith as she was hoisted into the air. *Now.* He had to do it now.

He began to whisper, dark words that carried on a low frequency that no one could hear. No one but the hyenas, the wild dogs so loyal to him because he was the one who fed them well. Who took care of them, who had made sure to keep them on his side. For such a day as this.

From far away, there was a yip, then another, then a third. Then the hyenas began to run. There was a clatter of nails on the porch, then a surprised gasp from Marie as the dogs barked and bit their way into the house.

Don't kill her, he whispered. *Save her for me.*

The dogs moved on, taking out whatever other obstacles remained in their way, snarling, biting, barking, and then they were coming down the stairs, the whole pack of them, running at full speed. Still, the coffin seemed to close in around Adrien, and he pushed at the sides, the top, knowing it was futile, trying all the same. *Hurry,* he told the hyenas. *Hurry.*

His frantic movements inside the coffin must have attracted the attention of Marie's army, because Adrien heard footsteps approach, then felt the leaden weight of a body land on top of the pine box. "Stay . . ." the body said, almost moaning the word. It had yet to learn to talk again, and all the vowels came out long and low.

Adrien shoved at the top, but nothing happened. He would never see Heather again. *Hurry, hurry,* he told the hyenas.

There was a growl, a bark, and then he heard the startled grunts of the zombies the hyenas attacked, followed by Meredith's muffled shrieks. A scramble of nails against the coffin, then a tearing of flesh, and the body that had weighted him down was dragged off, roaring in anger. Then, it went quiet as the dogs got their fill.

Adrien rocked to the left, then the right, then left again, harder each time, until the coffin tipped and clattered to the concrete floor. The impact shattered the wood and released him.

He scrambled out of the wooden prison and got to his feet. Meredith's eyes were wide above the gag, and she was kicking wildly against the chains, begging him to rescue her. He had no time nor desire to do so. He didn't need her and saw no reason to do anything other than leave her where she was. Soon, she would learn to conserve her energy and then maybe she'd last longer. Last long enough to see Heather become one of his kind.

Such a poor, pitiful thing, the sister. Still, he'd miss her when she was gone. She'd had fight in her, and that was one thing Adrien could admire. It would almost be a shame to kill her.

Almost.

But die she must, because his bride would be hungry when she awakened in her new form. How appropriate that their first meal together would be the one that would sever the last tie to her family.

CHAPTER 34

Terror washed over Heather in waves. She couldn't see. Couldn't hear. The darkness closed in on her, tight and fierce, coupled with the earthy scent of dirt and the musty smell of decay. Around her, she felt wood. Above her head, to the side of her, below her feet. She had to be in a box of some kind. She told herself it was a box, not a . . .

Oh God, a coffin.

She barely remembered being put in here. The bumpy journey from where she'd been to where she was. Her memory flashed to Adrien's mother, to her whispering something, and then someone grabbed her, banging her head against the wood. She'd drifted in and out of consciousness, but now she was awake. Aware.

And in serious trouble.

She pushed and kicked. Nothing happened. The wood refused to budge. The heat inside the small space quadrupled. Her lungs tightened. Was she running out of air? What if she couldn't get out? What if . . .

Heather opened her mouth and started to scream.

Now that Adrien had escaped the coffin, he had to plan how he would force Marie's cooperation. He needed to be careful, because it was clear she had resurrected the others to retake control. And what was worse, she now held what he wanted more than anything.

Heather. He had to find her. Now.

He called to the hyenas again, then to the vulture and the crows. In seconds, he had dispersed them again, the loyal creatures part of his hunting party. He would find Heather, and then he would make Marie pay. He only had to hope he wasn't too late.

He grabbed something he kept behind his house and then drove across town, moving fast while the hyenas trotted in the shadows beside him, noses to the ground. Suddenly, the vulture let out a cry, and the hyenas broke into a run. Adrien stepped on the gas and followed them. It didn't take him long to realize where they were headed.

The school.

He skidded to a stop outside the building, then jumped out of the car. The lights above him flickered. He slowed his pace, looked around. Playgoers were streaming into the auditorium, chatting and laughing. The hyenas let out a yip. Adrien glanced at the woods beside the school and saw what Marie had planned.

Zombies. Dozens of them, lurching toward the building. She wasn't going to take just Heather; she was going to take everyone.

The hyenas whined. Before Adrien could reach the front doors, the zombies were spotted by the others. A woman let out a scream, a man shouted, "What the hell?" and then the zombie pack began to descend. They attacked in a disorganized group, grabbing this one, that one, jerking from person to person. The screams became a loud wave carrying into the night.

Adrien didn't care. He broke through the crowd, running for the doors, calling Heather's name. He increased his stride, closing the distance until he was three feet, two feet, close enough to open the door—

Two figures stepped in front of him, colliding with Adrien. These zombies were bigger, stronger, than the ones in the cellar, and they took the blow from his body. The one on the right grabbed him and dragged him into the building.

Behind him, pandemonium had been unleashed, and from somewhere in the distance, he heard the sound of sirens. It was Boise and Panama all over again, only this time he knew it would be much, much worse.

"Now who's the stupid one?" Marie slipped in front of him. A woman trying to escape saw Marie's decaying body and tried to scream but froze. A zombie shoved her until she stumbled down the stairs and away. "I knew exactly where you were going."

"You won't keep me from her." Adrien tried to jerk out of the zombie's grasp, but the tall, thick creature held tight. The other one cemented a hand on Adrien's opposite shoulder. Marie was turning his own kind against him. Outside, the hyenas whined, barked, yipped.

"She's mine, Adrien." A smile curved up Marie's mouth. "Want to see?"

Before he could respond, the zombies dragged him down the hall, down the stairs, deep into the bowels of the school. Here, the air was musty, thick with the smell of the old furnace, molding textbooks, and forgotten purpose. Slivers of moonlight slipped through several egress windows. In the shadows lay a long wooden box. "Heather!" He lunged for it, but the zombies held him back.

Outside the windows, Adrien saw the hyenas pacing. He could still hear the screams of the humans, the battle with the zombies. The sirens whoop-whooped, but he knew it was too late for those people. But not too late for Heather.

"Let her go!" he said to Marie.

"Of course, Adrien. Why wait any longer and delay the inevitable?" Marie waved at one of her henchmen. He yanked back the lid of the coffin. Heather exploded up and scrambled out of it—and straight into the waiting trap of the zombie's arms. She struggled, kicking, screaming, biting, but she was no match for the stronger, bigger man.

Now! Adrien ordered the wild dogs. The hyenas leaped forward, throwing their bodies against the glass with a vicious fury that shattered first one window, then another. But as the dogs flowed down into the basement, the zombies seemed to expect the attack. One by one, they reached out and snapped the hyenas' necks. The dogs shrieked, whimpered—

And died.

His precious pets. They'd killed the beasts that had been so loyal to him and that had now sacrificed their lives for him. Fury rose inside Adrien and he lunged for Marie, even as the zombies held him back. "I will kill you for this!"

"No, you won't." Marie smiled. "Instead, you will watch as I kill her."

CHAPTER 35

My arms were on fire. My legs had gone dead. I cried until there were no tears left in me, screamed until my throat burned, even though no one could hear me through the gag. I was in the cellar, hanging from the ceiling just like that old man. What was going to happen to me? Would they kill me, one tiny, excruciating, painful piece at a time?

I kicked, searching for a wall, a box, a pole, anything I could use for leverage to raise myself up. My toe brushed something—what, I couldn't tell—and I kicked forward, then back again. A second time, I nicked the surface. I swung my body, biting into the gag as the manacles cut into my wrists in long, thin slices. Finally, my feet connected, landed on something.

A crate, it felt like, though I couldn't turn my head enough to see. I tiptoed back, and the wooden box rocked precariously. But each half step I managed brought my lower body up and released the agonizing pressure on my arms. The pain eased, and for the first time since they'd strung me up in the cellar, I could think.

I needed to get out of here. Needed to get to my sister before they did. The window was only a few feet away, but it might as well have been on another planet. Even if I swung like Tarzan, I couldn't get my body across the room and up into the small space of the window.

I shifted my wrists in the manacles and again had to bite down to keep from screaming as the metal rubbed against the fresh cuts. The cuffs were tight—tight enough that I couldn't slip out of them—and at least an inch and a half, maybe two inches, thick, not like modern cop cuffs, but like ones you'd see in a Frankenstein movie or something.

In the dark, I knew there were bodies around me. I hadn't seen, but I had heard—oh, I had heard—the dogs attacking those creatures. Adrien had to have been controlling them, and why he didn't set them on me, I didn't know. Before he left, he'd stopped and stared at me, then left me hanging here. For a later snack? I didn't want to be here to find out. *Bastard.*

But now there was only silence. Adrien and the dogs had left, and the angry shouts of his mother and the others had stopped. It was clear she was no longer working with

Adrien—the way he'd been thrown down here said that. The question was whether that boded well for me.

Or put me in twice as much danger.

I heard a car stop, the door slam, someone coming in the front door. Footsteps. And then, the basement door opening and someone coming down the stairs.

I started to scream and couldn't stop.

They had Heather pinned down across the coffin. She struggled but to no avail. Two held her arms, one held her legs, and over her mouth, Marie began to breathe. No, not breathe—*inhale*.

Adrien struggled against the two more who had been called in to hold him in place. They had him pressed into the wall, making sure he couldn't move, but he could see. Oh, he could see, see everything Marie was doing to his precious Heather. She was turning her, killing her, even as he watched. And there was nothing he could do to stop her.

Marie sucked the girl's breath out of her chest so hard, Heather's back rose off the coffin. Then she fell back down, limp, still. Quiet.

Dead? He couldn't tell, not from here, but he saw no movement coming from her chest, heard no sounds of her breathing. Had Marie taken her soul? Taken her last breath? Left her body empty, ready now for Marie to step in and inhabit the shell? All she had to do was breathe her own soul into Heather's—

And his precious love would become Marie's new host body.

No, not his Heather. *No.*

Marie turned to Adrien, triumph on her face. Already she looked younger, renewed as if the victory had restored her. "Oh, it's going to be so, so sweet, taking her body. Knowing you will look at this"—she swept a hand over Heather's immobile form—"and know it's me inside. Not this stupid girl you *love.*" She laid a sarcastic emphasis on the last word, then laughed. "That's the price you'll pay for betraying me, Adrien. For thinking you were smarter than me."

He lunged forward, but the zombies slammed him back, so hard he heard a bone splinter. Which one, he didn't know. Didn't care. "Leave her alone!"

There was a clatter upstairs, then a thunder of footsteps. "Everybody freeze!"

Adrien turned. A half dozen cops stood at the bottom of the stairs, weapons drawn, faces severe. They'd assessed the situation—young girl being held down against her will— and thought they could control it. They were wrong.

Two of the zombies working for Marie moved toward the cops. The uniforms shouted at them to freeze, but they kept going, spurred on by the orders of the one who had resurrected them. The cops fired once, twice, but they didn't know what they were dealing with. The undead would not be taken down by mere bullets. The zombies kept coming at the cops, even as more gunfire flew. They reached out, grabbed the police, and slammed the men, one by one, into the wall. In seconds, it was over, and Heather's human rescuers lay still.

A latecomer came charging down the stairs. "What's going on here?"

One of the zombies holding Adrien released him and stumbled forward, his steps still as ungainly as a new baby's. He yanked the cop up, pinning his arms behind his back. The man struggled, but the zombie held tightly. The cop looked around, saw his colleagues on the ground, and fought against the restraints, screaming at them that he was the police, but no one cared.

Marie came forward. She swiped a hand across the man's cheek, leaving a trail of deep, bloody scratches. He screeched in pain. Marie laughed. "Don't be afraid. With so many of us here, you'll go quickly. It'll be like a buffet."

With a shout, the cop flung off the zombie's hold, and as his arm came up, his fist slammed into Marie's hand, sending her dried fingers scattering like marbles. The zombies roared in anger at the attack on their leader.

They were distracted. His best opportunity was now. Adrien twisted and at the same time grabbed an arm of the one still holding him. He pulled his hands in opposite directions, sharp, hard, until he heard the satisfying sound of breaking bone. The zombie let out a shriek and tried to counter with his other arm, but it was too late. Adrien had already slid out of his grasp. He kicked out, hearing another crunch when his foot made contact with the zombie's knee. The big man yowled, then crumpled to the floor.

Still, the zombie kept coming, crawling across the floor with one arm, one leg, reaching for Adrien. Adrien deftly stepped out of the zombie's reach, then behind Marie. She turned, and the cop jerked toward Heather, rescue written all over his face. He was going to take her. Grab her body and take her away from Adrien. But Adrien couldn't let that happen. He released Marie, then grabbed a crowbar from the floor. "You can't have her! She's mine!"

And with that, he plunged the metal stem into the cop's chest.

CHAPTER 36

Meredith! Are you down here?" Sam's voice washed over me like a sweet wave. I jerked against my chains, cried into the gag. "I can't find the light switch but I hear you. I'm coming." Footsteps, shuffles, Sam's voice in the dark. "It's okay, I'm here. I'm here."

Something moved. A flicker in the corner, and then a groan.

"Meredith?" Sam's voice sounded too far away.

There was a shuffle, a grunt, then clattering as something collided with a stack of boxes. The creature crossed the cellar floor with dragging, staggered steps. The thing was panting, clearly hurt, but determined to keep going. It wasn't Sam, that I knew. That meant it had to be—

One of the walking dead. Not so dead now, after all.

I tried to scream through the gag. "Sam, watch out! There's one of them still in here."

Sam couldn't understand me, but he must have sensed the urgency.

The thing stopped moving. Stopped panting. Listening, I was sure. I smelled the zombie before I saw him. The stench of death, and then a half-rotted face looming out of the shadows.

I tried to scream Sam's name, but the creature only laughed. He sniffed the air around me, then licked his dry, leathery lips. "So hungry," he said, his voice low, guttural. "Mine."

I heard a cry, the exchange of punches. A clunk, a grunt, and then someone fell to the floor. I didn't utter a sound. I didn't want to know.

But then his hands were on my wrists, a tender touch working at the manacles. "It's okay. I hit him with a pipe. He's done. Let's get you out of here."

I nodded and collapsed into his arms, free from the gag at last. "Thank God you came, Sam."

He ran a hand over my hair and pressed a kiss to my head. "When you ran out of the school like that, I went looking for you, but I couldn't find you anywhere. So finally I went back to the school, and when you didn't show up for the play, I knew you had to be in trouble. That meant here." He grabbed me, held me to him. "I'm so glad you're okay."

"Me too, Sam," I whispered, then hugged him again. "Me too."

At that moment, the moon shifted outside and sent a ray of light into the basement, illuminating bodies everywhere. In the corner, a familiar pattern of horizontal stripes. *Don't let it be her,* I whispered as I pulled at the fabric. *Don't let it be her . . .*

Half an arm tumbled out of the housedress and rolled across the floor and onto my feet. An arm I recognized. It was Mrs. Cross. Or what was left of her.

I sucked back a shriek and scurried back. Oh God, oh God. She would never sit on her porch again. Never do that little harrumph thing. Never talk to her sister Celeste. I should have kept on calling the cops until they'd done a real investigation. Should have done more than I had. Now my neighbor was dead, and my sister was God only knows where with those insane people. I looked at Sam and he nodded. We both raced to the stairs.

The cop lay on the floor, blood seeping out of his wound. The crowbar stuck up out of the space above his heart. The other zombies circled around his body. Adrien sensed their hunger, their anticipation to have this ready, warm meal. They looked to Marie, waiting for their leader's permission to dine.

She scooped up Heather's body and cradled it against her chest, favoring her one unhurt arm. "You're too late, you fool. And now you will pay for your betrayal. I am done with you, Adrien." She spun away. "Kill him."

At that, the remaining four zombies turned on Adrien. There was no code of honor in this world Adrien inhabited, no loyalty to those like himself. There was only a leader and the leader's orders. Which meant his only way out was to become the leader.

His gaze fastened on Heather's limp, immobile body as Marie headed out of the basement room. Defeat filled him, weakened his stance. Why should he fight? Why not let them kill him? His only reason for continuing this worthless existence had died. Better to join her in death than to live through this and go on for centuries alone.

The zombies came toward him, hunger and hatred in their eyes. He was a threat to their leader, and they would do what it took to eliminate him. He would die the way he had lived—

Eaten by his own kind.

Goodbye, Heather. I love you.

As the first one made contact, Adrien told himself not to resist, to let it happen. To die, just as Romeo had when he had found his precious Juliet in that coffin. But then he remembered—maybe too late—that Romeo had been wrong. Juliet had been only feigning death.

And Romeo had died in vain.

CHAPTER 37

I had never seen Sam drive so fast to school. Neither of us talked about what we'd seen in the cellar. I think we were both trying to get a handle on it, to put it together with the very real world around us. And we were both hugely worried about Heather.

Sam screeched to a stop outside the building. Police cars surrounded Jefferson High, and people were running out of the school, screaming. Zombies staggered after them, jerking people to the ground, taking bites out of arms, legs.

"Oh my God," Sam said. "What the hell is going on?"

"I think Adrien and his mother awakened these things. Somehow." I shook my head. Putting together the pieces didn't matter, not really. "We have to get to my family."

The twins loomed up out of the darkness, and relief filled me. Two members of my family, safe. Then one of them jerked at my door handle, yanking the door open. "Get out," he said, his voice low and dark. Not Ted's/Tad's at all.

I started to protest, but he grabbed my arm, hauled me out of the car. The other twin did the same to Sam, and with strength I never knew they had, they hauled us past the cop cars, the screaming people, the pursuing zombies. We were dragged up the school stairs and into the building, down the hall, then through the doors of the auditorium. We fought against them, trying to get them to loosen their grip, digging our feet in against the ground, but it did no good. The twins had superhuman strength and a stony determination. They threw us to the floor by the stage, then stood close by, preventing us from escaping. Wendell, Mr. Edwards, and the rest of the play's cast were huddled against the fake balcony, eyes wide with fear. Mr. Edwards's arm and neck were bleeding. He had a hand pressed against the wound on his throat. A bite?

"Get out of here, Meredith," Mr. E. said, his voice weak and scared. "Bring back help."

"No one's leaving," one of the twins said. "Not until Adrien has Heather."

Has Heather? I glanced at Sam, and both of us knew that meant something terrible. Something neither of us wanted to picture. I scrambled to my feet, but before I could get away, one of the twins grabbed me. I strained against him, but it was useless. "Heather! Heather!"

I finally wrested my arms away. The twins stood there staring at me, blank, confused looks on their faces.

Were they zombies? Or just under some freaky spell?

"What on earth is happening?" Sam slipped into place beside me, his arm going around me like a shield. "What are we going to do?"

Before I could answer him, the black auditorium curtains parted and Adrien's mother stepped out onto the stage. Under the harsh lights, her decay horrified me. Her rotted skin still peeled off in chunks, exposing white bone and desiccated tendons. Her mouth was a slanted, drooling cavern.

Heather lay still in her arms. I prayed she was unconscious and not dead. The older woman spoke some words in a language I didn't understand, and several zombies came up, took my sister's body, and laid it on the funeral slab set up for Juliet.

As if she was dead.

I screamed and lunged for my sister's body, but one of the zombies shoved his rotted body between us and held me against his suit-jacketed chest. The smell of death choked my nostrils, made my stomach turn. I jerked against the zombie, kicking out with my foot as I did. The sickening sound of crunching bone filled the air, and the zombie crumpled but didn't let go.

Two others had grabbed Sam, and the rest were keeping

guard around Wendell, Mr. E., and the cast. The twins just stood there, stone-faced. Across from me, Adrien's mother laughed. "Give up now, and we'll eat you first. And as a special gift," she said, taking a step toward me, "we'll make it fast so you suffer less."

"No! Get away from me!" I jerked away from the zombie, kicking him again. He let out a roar, and then, just as I thought I would escape his clutches, I felt the sharp bite of teeth sinking into my arm. Blood gushed in pulses and dripped from the zombie's jaws. I stared at the crimson river running down my arm. Had that thing taken a freaking *bite* out of me?

He stared at me, as if deciding on the next appendage to savor. "More food," he said.

The pain kicked in and seared through the haze in my brain, jerking me into action. *Fight, Meredith, or die.* Outside the school, I heard screaming, gunfire. All too far away, too late.

"You're done dining here, psycho!" I swung back as hard as I could, wrenching out of his grasp. My body plowed into his, knocking him over. As he pinwheeled back, he grabbed at me, and I could feel myself going down, down, down with him.

Then a cracking sound, and the zombie released his hold. I tumbled to the floor and saw Wendell standing over the zombie, a piece of wood from the set in his hands. "Leave her alone!" he screamed, waving the stick.

"Wendell, look out!"

He wheeled around, but not fast enough. Another zombie—an old man dressed in flannel and jeans, his feet bare, his face a rotting, peeling thing—descended on Wendell in one swift move and bit into his neck.

Adrien's mother grabbed Wendell's face and seemed to kiss him. It made no sense, until I saw Wendell's cheeks sink in and hers expand. Was she sucking out his brains? His life? Whatever it was, it wasn't good. I scrambled forward, grabbing her ankles, yanking, pulling, but she held her ground. Then another pair of hands joined mine—Sam, always there when I needed him—and together, we got her off Wendell. He collapsed, crumpling like a rag doll. But it was too late. She had gotten him.

Then Adrien's mother fell onto the stage with a thud. I got to my feet and ran for Heather. My bleeding arm pounded out my pulse. I prayed it was a flesh wound and that the thing hadn't severed an artery.

Adrien's mother began to laugh, the sound of it like nails on a chalkboard. "How sweet. You're going to join your sister in death. She'll be the meal and you'll be the dessert."

"Shut up!" Sam roared, and backhanded her. She fell backward but popped right up, like one of those punching bags. Then the zombies descended, tearing Sam away from her and dragging him back into the shadows of the stage.

I couldn't help him. Couldn't do anything but scramble over to my sister's body, lying so cold and still on the flower-covered slab. The main course for a sick, twisted meal.

"Get away from her! She's mine. Just mine!"

It was the voice—Adrien's mother's voice—that roused Heather. The last thing she remembered was seeing that woman leaning over her, opening her mouth. And then, oh God, what she'd seen inside that mouth—

Death, crawling and squirming in and out of that black toothless cavity. Worms and bugs, beetles and flies. Like an infestation, all inside her throat.

After that, Heather had heard sounds, so many of them, but she'd been tired, beyond exhausted, and it had been easier to sleep. All she remembered was being picked up and carried somewhere else.

Whatever had drugged her was beginning to wear off. She still couldn't move—her limbs felt as heavy as tree trunks—but she could hear. She opened her eyes and the ceiling above her swam into focus. Where was she?

She flicked her gaze left and right. She glimpsed painted trees. A wooden balcony. She heard people screaming, the constant whoop-whoop of sirens. It took a second, but then she realized she was at school. Lying in the middle of the set for *Romeo and Juliet*.

Adrien.

Where was he? Was he one of them, too? She couldn't bear to think that. He had to be different, had to be. But the sinking feeling in her gut told her he was exactly the same. That she had been the fool who had believed him. The fool who was now going to end up dead.

"Let her go!" Meredith's voice. What was she doing here?

"Never!" Adrien's mother screamed. "Her body will become mine. Then you will be my first meal. Such sweet justice." She laughed. "But I must hurry, for already she stirs. The spell is wearing off. If she awakens fully, it will be too late for me to take over her body. And after I am done, I will feed the rest of your worthless family to my helpers."

Oh God. That was what she planned to do? Was that why Heather couldn't move? Adrien's mother had done something to paralyze her? But wait, if the spell was wearing off, then maybe that meant she'd be able to move soon.

From somewhere close, Heather heard thuds, steady and firm. Banging against a door.

"Oh, my new friends will want a piece of this. They're so hungry. That stupid old woman from across the street was merely a snack. Let's have them join us, shall we?" Adrien's mother said. There was a click, followed by the creak of a door opening, and then Heather saw even more of those zombie creatures step onto the stage. They were everywhere. *Oh God, no, no.*

Heather willed her fingers to flex, but nothing happened. She did it again, concentrating hard, and after what seemed like an eternity, she felt a flicker against her hip. She had moved! She did it again, focusing on her feet, her legs.

"Grab her!" Adrien's mother said. Meredith shrieked.

Heather turned her head and saw Meredith pinned against the wall, one zombie on either side, Adrien's mother zeroing in her. Meredith was going to die, and if Heather didn't do something, it would be all her fault. It already was. She was the one who had fallen for Adrien, who had trusted him. The betrayal stung sharp and hard, but she pushed it aside. Later, she'd deal with that. She had brought her family into this. Now she had to get them out.

Move, damn it, move. Her legs twitched, her arms flailed, and with each jerk, blood began to flow through her veins and she could feel herself coming alive again. *Move faster. Get off this table. Get over there. Stop them.*

She closed her eyes, concentrated, and put every bit of effort into moving to the side. She slid off the table, landing on her feet. No one noticed. They were too busy taunting Meredith.

"Where shall I start?" Adrien's mother ran a hand down

Meredith's cheek. Meredith flinched. "With this sweet face? Or here?" She touched her arm, skimming over an open wound. "Should I finish the job started by another?"

"Leave her alone!" Heather shoved off from the table and lunged at Adrien's mother. She was still unsteady on her feet, and instead of grabbing her, she fell into her. The two of them tumbled to the floor.

Adrien's mother lashed out with everything—her mouth, her fingers, her feet. Heather held on, pinning her to the floor, but Adrien's mother was bigger and stronger. She bucked Heather off not just once, but twice. Heather climbed right back on top, using the dead weight of her body to pin the other woman down. With a roar, the zombies reached out for Heather, but she shifted away from the slower-moving creatures and they accidentally grabbed Adrien's mother instead. Three times they played this game until Adrien's mother scrambled forward—toward the zombies—and Heather didn't get off fast enough. She was snatched up and tossed to the side like a rag doll, immediately held captive by two more zombies. She watched, helpless, as the zombies slammed Meredith onto the table. They stood over her, drool pouring from the sides of their mouths, clearly anticipating their next meal, Wendell right in front, one of them now. But Meredith was too fast for them, and she crawled off the table, kicking out, connecting with one of the zombie's knees, bringing him to the ground. A punch into the throat of another, and he staggered back, giving her enough room to run past them and over to Heather.

She heard the auditorium doors bang open, followed by the dull thud of marching. More of them were coming. Oh God. It was hopeless.

Then she caught a familiar scent and froze. Was it . . . ? Impossible. But no, it was there. Unmistakable. The scent of Old Spice.

Heather raised up on one elbow. "Dad?"

A figure stomped forward. Heather froze. She knew that suit. That tie. She'd last seen them eight months ago—

In her father's coffin.

Heather looked at Meredith, and in that moment, she saw the reflection of the same thoughts.

The zombie brought in to execute the Willis girls would be none other than their own father.

CHAPTER 38

My father bypassed Heather and went for me first. Before I could deal with the shock of seeing him among the walking dead, my father's hand went around my throat and he lifted me up until my feet dangled above the floor. His eyes stared straight ahead, not seeing me, not seeing anything at all. I clawed at his hand, kicked at his legs, but it was useless. "D-Dad . . ." I croaked out. "D-Dad . . . it's m-m-me."

No reaction. "D-D-Dad! P-p-please . . ."

Heather pummeled the zombies holding her, trying to get away. "Dad! It's us! Stop!"

Adrien's mother began to laugh. "Oh, isn't this perfect? I had no idea he was your father. But how appropriate that the one who will crush your worthless throat is the same one who brought you life."

I didn't listen to her. I couldn't. If I believed her, I would fall apart. I shifted in his grip until I could force the words out. "Dad! Dad! It's Meredith!"

Adrien's mother whispered in my father's ear. "Kill her. Then we shall dine on her together."

My father's hand tightened around my throat. The room began to swim in front of me.

"Daddy!" Heather cried. "Daddy, stop! Please! Oh God, Daddy, I'm sorry!"

His grip slackened, and light dawned in his eyes. I gulped in some air and felt my feet touch the floor. The dad thing released me, pivoted toward Heather. She was sobbing, straining against the ones holding her back, calling for my father over and over again, telling him she was sorry. That she hadn't meant it. That she wished it had been she who'd died.

He took a step toward Heather, then another and a third, his movements jerky, slow, heavy. Adrien's mother swatted at his shoulder. "Get back here! Kill this worthless piece of—"

My father punched her so hard, her lower jaw went flying across the room. She shrieked, a garbled mess of a sound. She crawled after the piece of bone and shoved it back into her mouth, but it fell out again.

My father plodded over to Heather. She hung limply in the zombies' arms, crying so hard that her entire body shook. "I'm sorry, Daddy. I'm sorry."

The thing that was my father, and wasn't, lifted a hand and brushed the hair away from Heather's face. "S'okay," he said, the word coming out long, slow, and guttural. "S'okay."

She looked up at him, tears streaming down her face. "I love you, Daddy."

Something that resembled a smile came over my father's face, and then he turned and grabbed the zombie holding Heather's left arm. He clamped down on the creature's wrist until the thing let out a yowl and released her. Then he flung the creature away and did the same to the one on Heather's other side. Free, she ran sobbing into his arms. He remained stiff, as if this walking dead side of him didn't know what to do. "S'okay," he said again.

With a shriek, Adrien's mother lunged toward me. She yanked a knife out of her pocket, then pressed it to my throat. I cried, scared, so scared. My father headed toward me just as Adrien's mother shoved the knife into one of her minion's hands. The zombie took her place and pressed the blade deeper. Then Adrien's mother hurried over to Heather and opened her mouth over Heather's. I screamed as she began to breathe into Heather's mouth, not sucking out

Heather's life this time, but *invading* her body. My father hesitated, trying to choose a daughter to save.

The auditorium door flew open a second time. Adrien ran down the aisle with something red in his hand, something I'd seen before, and a flurry of bodies followed him—more zombies. More killers to join the party.

A minute ago, I'd thought we had a way out, a chance of surviving this.

Now I knew we didn't.

CHAPTER 39

Rage blinded Adrien to everything around him but Heather. He charged forward, dropping what he carried onto the floor. Ignoring the others, he yanked Marie away from Heather. His fingers sank deep into the soft, decaying skin of her arm until he reached bone. "You will not have her."

Marie pivoted toward him so fast that her arm snapped in half. The lower part clattered to the floor, fingers still twitching on a useless, severed forearm.

Adrien closed his hand around her throat. Her eyes bulged, her tongue flicked out, and the worms inside her began to scramble out.

She clawed at his wrist with her free hand, stripping it down to bare bone. Still Adrien held on, moving backward as he did, dragging the Marie hellcat with him until he reached the zombie holding the blade against Meredith's throat. The zombies did as he expected—they diverted their attention from Heather and her sister and began to cross the stage to rescue their leader. The other humans took the opportunity to run away, screaming for help as they charged out of the auditorium. Adrien paid them no attention. He grabbed the knife away from the zombie. The thing let out a confused grunt.

Just then, the ones that had been with him in the cellar, the ones that had been sent to kill him, the same ones he had turned into his own army by killing the biggest one first and establishing his authority, entered the auditorium from where they'd been waiting outside and joined the fight. "Take them down!" Adrien ordered.

The war began. He heard the tearing of body parts, the rising crescendo of angry roars as zombie turned on zombie, each fighting to survive. There were no rules in this kind of game. The only goal was to immobilize the opponent by tearing off his limbs, breaking the spinal column, ripping the head from its seat.

One lone zombie crossed toward Heather. Meredith followed him, and when she reached Heather, she dragged her sister into a hug while the zombie stood over them in a protective stance. *What the hell?* Adrien wondered.

Marie kicked out, her foot slamming into Adrien's knee. Adrien stumbled and got up but didn't release her neck.

Heather screamed. "Don't! Don't hurt him!"

He turned toward his precious love. "Get out of here," he said to Heather. Soon things would go from bad to worse and he wanted Heather to be safe. "You and your sister." Marie kicked again and again, shattering his thigh bone, his pelvis, sending him crashing to the floor and the knife skittering out of his reach. Adrien slammed Marie onto the stage, so hard her spine cracked. She went limp in his arms for a moment, then began to twitch again, refusing to stop. Soon, her zombies would break away and come after him, to try to save their leader.

In the next moment, he felt Heather's arms around him, pulling at him. "Adrien, come with me."

"I . . . I can't." He could run now, escape, but where would he go? He thought of the lonely, painful existence he had suffered for the past ninety years.

He had thought having Heather with him would make it all okay. But as he felt her tears sink into his skin, he knew the price she would pay. All for his selfishness. She would walk the same path he had—and someday, maybe hate him for doing that to her. He turned, one hand still on Marie's neck, the other coming up to swipe the tears from Heather's face. "I can't because . . . I love you. And for that reason, you must leave, Heather. Now."

"I love you," she sobbed. "I can't leave you."

He closed his eyes, and never in all the decades he had been this creature had he wished more to be human. "I know, my love."

Marie surged forward with one last effort and knocked the sunglasses from his face, as if to say, *See what your love truly is.*

Heather recoiled from the death in his eyes, the truth he had kept hidden behind those glasses all this time. He turned away, the pain of her rejection shooting through him, pain he'd never thought he could feel again.

"I love you," he said again, his strength waning now as his broken limbs took their toll. "Please don't remember me as a monster."

"Never. Never."

Marie let out a roar, and he heard the sound of her zombies responding, coming for him. "Heather, go. Before they kill you, too."

"Adrien!"

The zombies reached for him. He released Marie and felt her upper jaw sink into his skin. Before she could do more than graze him, the zombie that had been with Heather yanked Marie back, off Adrien.

"Daddy, don't!" Heather cried.

He didn't listen. The zombie Heather called her father tossed Marie aside. The pack under her control saw his intent and lunged for him. He shrugged them off, went to Marie, and curled his hands around Marie's throat. Even as the other zombies pulled at him, tearing flesh and breaking bones, he held on, until his hands came together in one massive squeeze—and Marie's head tumbled to the floor.

Dead. Again.

One of the zombies let out an angry yowl, yanked up the knife, and, in one swipe, cut all the way through Heather's father's throat. His severed head rolled into the corner, and then his body slumped to the floor, twitching for several seconds.

Heather started shrieking and crying. Her sister went to her. Then Sam crawled out of the shadows, bleeding badly. He draped a protective arm over the girls and they turned into him, averting their eyes from their dead father.

Adrien looked at the body and remembered back ninety years. To his father, his mother. He saw the pain in his Heather's face and knew he had caused it. He had caused all of this. And only he could end it.

"Go," he said to Heather, his voice hard, leaving no room for argument. "Go now."

Meredith and Sam tugged Heather to her feet. A moment later, the three of them were gone. His love was safe.

Adrien scrambled down to the auditorium floor, his broken body moving in jerks and fits. He grabbed the red container he had kept hidden outside the house—a part of him had always known this day would come. Then he dragged his battered body back up to the stage and waited for them to come. As they did, he depressed the sprayer.

Acid spewed in an arc over the zombies. They screamed, and then their bodies began to smoke, shrivel, and dissolve into puddles, no chance of ever being resurrected again. Beside him, he saw the twins waiting for instructions. Their glassy gaze wavered—the spell was beginning to wane. "You are free," he said. "Go. Go now."

The boys started, and then their faces filled with awareness. They took one look at the carnage around them, then began to run. There was a scream, and the boy from history class—no longer a boy, but a zombie like him—dived for the twins. "Leave her family alone!" Adrien shouted, then depressed the button and watched the boy disappear into nothing more than a crumpled pile.

Adrien crawled over to the last body and pushed the button again. Under the stream, Marie's body began to smoke, then blur into something unrecognizable. Something like regret filled him for the way it had to end.

"Freeze!"

Adrien turned and saw the guns, the angry faces trained on him.

I love you, Heather.

Then he turned the sprayer toward himself and held the button until his fingers dissolved.

His last thought before he died was of Heather. He held on to the image of her smile and her deep brown eyes until the acid consumed him and took him back to the grave.

CHAPTER 40

It wasn't easy getting these past the nurse gestapo, you know." I pulled the fast food bag out of my jacket and placed it on Sam's hospital tray.

"Thanks. I was getting totally sick of rubber chicken and Jell-O." He dug into the bag and pulled out the packages of fries. All three of them. He grinned. "Do you expect me to share?"

I plopped down onto the bed beside him. "Of course. Call it a finder's fee."

He laughed, then spread the bag out on the tray, dumping all the fries onto the paper. I fished the ketchup and salt packets out of my pocket, sprinkling a ton of salt on one side of the fries, just a dash on his. Creating a mountain of ketchup in the middle.

"How are you doing?" I asked.

"Better. Doctor said I was lucky those things didn't hit any major organs. Most of the wounds were flesh wounds, but this one is going to leave a hell of a scar." He pointed to his arm, where the bandages bulged beneath his hospital gown.

"Me too." I showed him my own bandage on my arm, and we didn't talk for a moment, just stared at each other with disbelief and gratitude that we were here at all to compare scars. Then I counted my blessings for the four hundredth time in the past few days. After Heather and I escaped from the auditorium, Adrien had apparently killed the rest of the zombies. The place was a mess—filled with decaying body parts and puddles of acid everywhere. The principal had said it would be at least a year before the auditorium was in any shape to be used again. That was okay. I didn't think anyone was much interested in revisiting that space.

Or what had happened there.

The heat wave had broken and the town had gone on, acting as if it had been some freak event. If people talked about it, they said it was some crazy gang that had gone and dug up dead bodies for unspoken purposes. It wasn't the truth, of course, but if a lie made it easier to handle that half the cemetery had come to life and tried to kill the students and staff of Jefferson High School . . . why not?

I did, however, mention that I'd seen the neighbors burying a briefcase. That brought out the cadaver dogs, who had a field day in the backyard, finding the bones of the businessman, the old guy, and some woman who had disappeared walking home from work. They'd found Mrs. Cross in the basement, too. The newspaper was still filled with headlines such as "Serial Killers in Our Midst?" Heather and I saw the paper and just exchanged knowing glances.

My mother and Aunt Evelyn had escaped it all because the flower shop owner had been smart enough to lock the doors when he saw the crazy stuff going down. Heather and I were grateful that our family had come out okay. My mom had put her credit cards away, vowing we would have dinner as a family every night from there on out. She'd stuck to it, five out of the past six nights, skipping dinner only once to go to the mall sidewalk sale. But she took me and Heather, so it was still a family night. I figured that was a giant step in the right direction. Aunt Evelyn and the twins came out of their Adrien love-fest stupor, as did the rest of the school. I guess his being dead broke whatever spell he had had over everyone. This past weekend, Aunt Evelyn and the twins moved back to Minnesota. Cookies arrived in the mail, and the twins' last phone call was filled with only one topic: basketball. Life was as back to normal as it got for us.

"You doing okay?" Sam asked me. "You got pretty quiet there."

"Yeah, fine."

The grin curved across his face again. "Good. Because . . ." He paused, took in a breath and let it out. "I wanted to ask you out."

"Ask me . . ." I stared at him. "Out?"

"On a real date. To someplace that doesn't serve burgers." Even with his hair all rumpled and wearing the checked hospital gown, he looked sexy and cute at the same time.

"Say yes."

I turned and saw Heather in the doorway. Her cheeks were blooming with color, her eyes dancing with happiness. Despite Adrien dying, she seemed to have found herself again, as if everything she'd gone through in the past few weeks had closed some wound. "Hey, Heather."

She came into the room, dumping an enormous teddy bear onto the end of Sam's bed. "Tell him yes, Meredith. You like him, he likes you. The two of you should go out."

"But you—"

"We were more friends than anything," Heather said. She looked at Sam, and he nodded. "So stop letting the excuse of me get in your way and go out with him. He's a catch."

I grinned. "I know that."

Heather patted Sam's foot. "Just wanted to stop by and say hello. I'll catch you later." She ducked out of the room, shutting the door as she left.

"I think she wanted to leave us alone." Sam's voice dropped into a husky, sexy range.

I could hardly breathe. Especially when he looked at me like that. "Aren't you supposed to be resting?"

He reached out and tugged me closer to him, then tipped my chin until it was right beneath his. "That's why you'll do all the work when you kiss me."

I leaned in and did just that. Kissing Sam was the most wonderful thing in the world, I decided. He reached behind my head and tugged me closer, sending my pulse into overdrive.

Then he pulled back and grinned at me. "That was nice."

"Yeah." I sat up and smoothed a hand over his blanket. "Do you think something like that will ever happen again?"

"A kiss? I hope so."

"No, I meant . . ."

"I know what you meant," Sam said quietly. "But no. We're all wiser now. And besides, I think this place is done with tragedies."

"No more Romeo and Juliet?"

"I think it's time we wrote our own play, don't you?"

"Our own, huh?" I grinned.

"Yep. And this one will have a happy ending." His hand covered mine, warm and strong and safe. "I promise."

I looked into Sam's blue eyes, and all the worries that had been with me in the days since the attack disappeared. "Sounds like a plan, Mr. Shakespeare."

A. J. WHITTEN is a pseudonym for *New York Times* bestselling author Shirley Jump writing with her teenage daughter, Amanda. A shared love of horror movies and a desire to spice up the Shakespeare stories that are required reading in high schools led to their collaboration on *The Cellar* and their previous book together, *The Well*. Learn more at www.ajwhitten.com.